KIDS' KLASSICS

SPOTTED BOY
AND THE
COMANCHES

Mabel Earp Cason

Pacific Press® Publishing Association
Nampa, Idaho

Dedication

To those young folks who first heard this story related and contributed their suggestions: Jeanne, Phyllis, Marshall, Joelle, Gregory, Laura, Richard, Betty Rae, David, Douglas, and Jimmy; also to Elizabeth Anne, Margaret, Mary Patricia, and Karen, this book is lovingly dedicated by their grandmother.

Cover image: Ed Guthero
Interior art: James Converse

Copyright 1963 by
Pacific Press® Publishing Association

Library of Congress Catalog Card No. 63-21055

Litho in U.S.A.

Additional copies of this book may be purchased at
http://www.adventistbookcenter.com

ISBN 978-0-8163-1331-0

October 2022

Contents

Little-bit

OLD Thad Conway sat on his front porch and rocked, while he called to mind the happenings and the people of years long gone. What took place when he was just a boy seemed more clear in his recollections than what had happened only yesterday.

There was the day when Thad's father had brought home the little Spanish mare. The whole family had gathered around the wagons as father and sixteen-year-old Travis drove in. They had gone to Waco to buy supplies as they did once every year.

They had bought flour and cornmeal, beans and dried fruit and lard. This time they had also bought a new gun and plenty of ammunition. They had bought bolts of calico for mother Conway's dresses and for summer dress shirts for Thad and Travis and their father, as well as hickory cloth for their work shirts and gray wool jean cloth that mother would make into breeches for them.

They had bought a new iron stove for mother to cook on in

place of the fireplace she had used ever since she and father had come to central Texas and started this ranch. Thad had never forgotten how she ran admiring fingers over its smooth blackness nor how the tears of happiness shone in her eyes. He had been happy for her.

Waco was 120 miles away, and father and Travis had been gone three weeks. The very first sight Thad's eyes had taken in when they drove into the yard was what was tied to the tail gate of Trav's wagon.

"Why, pa!" he exclaimed. "Where did you get that miserable old crowbait?" She was the sorriest-looking specimen of horse-flesh he had ever seen. Thad loved horses more than most people and always would, but more than that, a horse was very important to boy, man, or woman on the western frontier of Texas in the year 1863.

"Why, she can hardly stand up!" When Thad patted her mud-encrusted nose, she nickered weakly and rolled gentle eyes toward him. His heart went out to her right then and there, poor specimen though she appeared to be. Tears of pity rose to his eyes, but they remained unshed. Thad was twelve years old and such a big boy simply did not cry.

There was a jagged white scar on the little mare's left hip that looked like a pair of opened scissors. It appeared as though it might have been a brand, but the boy examined it and found it to be a scar from some old injury. It would serve as a mark by which to recognize his pony. She was his, for pa had said, "She's all yours, son."

"She looks mighty near starved," Thad said.

"Indians had her," Trav explained. "We got her off of some Rangers this side of Waco. They had had a brush with some Comanches a while back. After the Indians took off, the Rangers followed them a little way, and they found this Spanish mare. The Comanches had turned her loose because she was played out. They had ridden her down like Indians do."

"I reckon they stole her off of some white settlers," Thad guessed.

"Of course they did," Travis agreed. "Maybe from some of those Spaniards down in Mexico. Might have killed off the family, too."

"One of the Rangers felt sorry for her and fed and watered her," father Conway explained, "but he couldn't keep her, so I took her off his hands."

"How much did you give him for her?" Reed asked. Reed was Thad's eldest brother and he was a Texas Ranger as Thad hoped someday to be. Now he was at home for a week nursing a crippled arm. He had taken an arrow in it while fighting with some Comanches a few days before.

"The Ranger was having some blacksmithing done when we went to have Star and Jerry shod, and he said he would let me have the pony for the price of his blacksmithing. It was four bits."

"Fifty cents!" Mother and Reed both laughed. Reed said, "I figure you got yourself beat out of fifty cents at that. What made you buy her?"

"The fellow told me she seemed gentle, and I figured that Thad here would like to have her. He's so tenderhearted about animals."

"Those little Spanish ponies are tough and wiry," Trav remarked, "even though they are not very big. She's not old, either; three or four years at the outside, is my guess."

Thad looked closer at the little mare and saw that her mane and tail, now full of cockleburs, would be long and thick when curried. Her hide would be black and shining when it was healed of the skinned places and had the mud brushed from it and a little fat built in under it. He loved the little mare from that minute.

He spent the rest of the afternoon rubbing the mud from her and putting salve on her cuts and skinned places. Then he curried her coat until it shone. She loved the attention. He petted her and talked in gentle tones into her ear and she seemed to fall in love with the boy, as he had with her.

Thad's dog, Whizzer, a big old yellow hound without much ancestry to speak of, sat and watched the whole proceeding. Thad had to pet him a little now and then, too, for he did not want him to be jealous.

3

Spotted Boy and the Comanches

That night, just before bedtime, the family were still joking father Conway about buying the little mare.

"Well, she'll be pretty when Thad gets through with her," he said. "Some say those Spanish horses have Arabian blood in them. That's why her eyes are so big, her nostrils so wide, and her ankles so slender."

"She sure is a little bit of a thing," mother remarked.

"Little-bit!" Thad jumped from his chair and shouted the words. "That's what I'll call her, Little-bit."

"One thing I forgot to tell you, Thaddy," his father said. "The fellow said that she can smell Indian farther than a hound can smell a rabbit. So when you're away from the house, you watch her and she'll let you know if any Indian is nigh."

*   *   *

Mother and father Conway were both born in Missouri, which was frontier country in those days, but they were from restless stock that kept moving along toward the west every generation in the hope of bettering themselves. That's how America got itself settled up.

Everybody knows that Mexico and Texas used to belong to Spain. Later, when Mexico won her revolt against Spanish rule in 1821, she took Texas with her. Moses Austin got permission from the new Mexican governor of Texas to bring in three hundred families of settlers from the United States across the Sabine River. Soon afterward he died, but his son, Stephen F. Austin, went ahead with his plans. Both of Thad Conway's grandfathers, grandpa Wilson and grandpa Conway, were among those first settlers in Texas, where they made their home beside the Brazos River. There Louisa Wilson and Sampson Conway grew up together as neighbors and were married. From the day they had come to Texas both families and their neighbors had fought Comanches.

After their first two children were born, Samps and Louisa Conway got that same crowded feeling that had made their ancestors itch to move, so they traveled farther west to the extreme frontier in Brown County. Here they had established this ranch on the banks of the Pecan Bayou, a dark stream that wound between deep banks where tall pecan and elm trees kept it in perpetual shade.

That was in 1851, and the Comanches, who were constantly being pushed farther west, had been kicking up trouble ever since. Horse stealing was their most frequent offense against the white settlers, but house burning and murder were also among their accomplishments, embellished by a kidnaping now and then.

"For two years after we moved here," Thad had often heard his mother say, "I never laid eyes on another white woman. There were a few footloose young men but no women here on the frontier. I was a happy woman, I can tell you, when Tom and Ellie Clark moved in two miles up the creek." She and Ellie Clark had become fast friends and would remain so all their lives.

Talk around the fireplace or on the front porch at the Double Bar O Ranch was most often of Comanches and their ways. Sometimes these days it was of the war between the states that was going on far to the east of Texas. Few of the men from this part of the state had left for the war, though Texas was now a part of the United States, having fought with Mexico to gain her independence. Every able-bodied settler on the western frontier was needed for protection against the raiding Comanches.

One spring evening when the breeze from the faraway gulf was blowing soft and gentle and the chill had gone from the air, Reed remarked, "Any moonshiny night now you can expect the Comanches to raid you. I'll have to join my Rangers tomorrow, but you ought to be fairly safe with Ben Atkins and Tom Weaver and Charlie Bynum here with you. Ma and Travis and Thad are pretty good with a rifle, too."

"Where do you suppose they hide out when they are not raiding?" Thad asked.

"They do very well, young'un," Reed answered. "The United States Government has given them territory up beyond the Red River in The Nations."

"Is that what you call 'Indian Territory'?" Thad asked.

"That's it," his brother answered. "The Government feeds them and gives them clothes if they will stay there, and most of the tribes are satisfied to stay. But the Comanches are a wild bunch. When the weather is warm enough, they move down into west Texas and steal from the settlers along these creeks."

"That's why they don't bother us in the winter," Thad guessed.

"That's the reason. Old Yellow Cloud is supposed to be the chief of the band that does the raiding in this part of the country. The Rangers have been on the lookout for his hideout way out west of here for a long time now."

"If you could find them, would you get back some of our horses they have stolen?" Thad inquired.

"Young'un," Reed replied, "by the time we catch up with those horse thieves they have driven them clear across the border into New Mexico and sold them to the Comancheros. The Comancheros sell them down into Old Mexico and there our brands don't mean a thing. Our horses are gone—for good."

As summer came on that year of 1863, the raids commenced. The Fairless family over on Lonesome Creek, fifteen miles away, was wiped out, with the exception of one fourteen-year-old boy who was away from home at the time. By the first of July the Comanches had raided the Conways' Double Bar O Ranch on two different occasions, stealing horses each time. There seemed to be a member of the raiding band that had taken a fancy to Little-bit, for on both occasions she was among the horses stolen.

Thad's dog Whizzer and Travis's hunting hounds woke the family both times before the Indians had got away with more than a few head of stock, so Little-bit must have been snatched right at first. Both times she came back within a week or two, tired and dirty and hungry, her mouth sore and bleeding from the jaw rein the Indians used.

"I have a sneaking idea," said pa after the second time she was taken, "that these thieves must be a few young bucks, maybe in their teens, and one of them has taken a special liking to your pony." No one knew the ways of Comanches better than Samps Conway, so Thad felt that he must be right.

He kept his pony curried until her coat was shiny black and her mane and tail were as long and thick and soft as a woman's hair. He really could not blame that young Indian who wanted her for his own.

After the second time Little-bit was stolen, Thad fastened her outside the window of the room where he slept. He used a heavy chain to tie her to the thick log wall. That, he believed, would make it hard for anyone to steal her.

A week later, on a night when the moon rose at three in the morning, Thad heard Little-bit give a frightened snort. She was pawing at the wall, and the dogs were barking "Injun" as plain as they could. Thad seized his gun and leaped from his bed.

"Trav, Trav!" he yelled. "They're after Little-bit!" He ran to the window. The dogs were barking now down toward the creek bank where the barns and corrals were located. Little-bit was snorting and pulling at her chain.

Thad had started to follow Travis when he saw Ben Atkins and Tom Weaver come running from the bunkhouse. They were all heading in the direction the dogs had taken. But Thad wanted to make sure that Little-bit was secure and unharmed, so he stopped to look her over.

Five arrows hung from her body at crazy angles. His father joined him. He had not followed the others, for he said, "Those Indians may just be setting a trap by tolling the dogs away to get us to follow them. Then some others will attack here at the house."

Now as he looked at Little-bit, he said, "I reckon those Comanches have made up their minds that if they can't have your pony, they'll fix it so you can't have her either."

"Pa," Thad asked anxiously, "do you think she'll die from these arrows?"

"No, son," his father answered, as he worked one of them from her shoulder. "I don't think she's hurt very bad. She's losing a little blood, but she won't suffer any bad effects. Of that I'm sure. None of them has struck a vital part."

The others were coming back from the corrals. "They've gone,"

Spotted Boy and the Comanches

Ben Atkins said. "And I'd be willing to bet that it was only a couple of young braves trying to get Little-bit!"

*　　　*　　　*

Brown County, Texas, in those faraway days was a good place to live in spite of the danger, and no one dwelt too much on that except during the summer when the Comanches were active.

In the spring, with the flowers blooming for miles among the mesquite grass, filling the air with a drifty perfume, Thad's head was fairly set to spinning as he galloped through them on Little-bit.

Thad wore his gun whenever he left the house, winter or summer. Often as he started, he would hear his mother calling, "Thad, have you got your gun with you?"

It seems a strange thing for a mother to say to her twelve-year-old son. But no one—boy, man, or woman—dared go far from home without a gun in that part of Texas. One never knew when he might be jumped by Indians.

Then, there were snakes and bears. In winter there might also be a "loafer" wolf to shoot at. A calf or colt had small chance for his life when a wolf found him, so wolves were shot on sight.

New Neighbors

MOTHER Conway was dishing up the dinner of turnip greens, roast buffalo hump, and beans, and Thad was putting them on the table along with big pitchers of milk and buttermilk when they heard Mr. Conway riding into the yard.

Thad said, "Somebody's with pa, and it isn't Trav nor any of our hands."

"I wonder who it could be," Thad's mother said, taking the big pan of hot biscuits from her new oven. Just then his father came into the kitchen and, sure enough, a man and a boy were with him. The boy, dark and slim and unsmiling, appeared to be a year or two older than Thad. He seemed to be shy.

"Louisa," Mr. Conway said, "meet our new neighbor, Mr. Wiley Branson."

Thad stared at the boy, who stared back with level gaze. But neither of them spoke.

"This is my son, Beauford," Mr. Branson said. "Beau for short."

Each nodded, Thad's white head and Beau's black one bobbing in unison. "Howdy," each of them said.

The Conways had heard that a new family had moved in on the open range south about twelve miles, and they had been anxious to meet them. Louisa Conway and Ellie Clark had talked of going to visit the new lady. Women were a scarcity along the bayou in those days, although a good number of families had moved into the area. But they were widely scattered, and some of the ranches were being opened up by single men. So the womenfolk looked forward to getting together once or twice a year. They relied on any sort of excuse that could be thought up—any excuse, that is, good enough to induce the men to go with them. The men did not like the women to take the risk of riding far alone, because of Indians. There were also some white men in the country who could not be trusted entirely. This was still lawless country, the more so since the soldiers had been called away to take part in the war.

The Bransons sat down to dinner with the Conways and their hired help. Travis and Ben Atkins came in from the branding corral just as the meal started.

"Well, Mr. Conway," said Mr. Branson, "I see you've been on a buffalo hunt. How far did you have to go?"

"Not more than a day's wagon ride," Mr. Conway said. "Closest they've come to our country for a good many years."

This part of the country was too heavily wooded in spots for the larger herds of bison to run in, but Samps Conway and his sons had been out on the plains a week ago and had brought home a whole wagonload of buffalo meat.

Thad would never forget anything that happened the day the Bransons had dinner with them. Seeing the first two members of the Branson family made it an important day for him, more so than he realized at the time.

Wiley and Beau Branson left soon after dinner.

"Now you-all come down and see us just as soon as you can, Mrs. Conway," Wiley said as they were leaving. "Marcella gets mighty lonesome. She's never been very far away from her own kin before, and she isn't taking it too well. Her folks are all back in Kentucky except one sister who lives in San Antonio."

"We'll be down just as soon as Ellie Clark and I can get our men-folk to go with us," Louisa Conway promised.

"You come, too," Beau said to Thad. Although he had said little since coming into the house, Thad had felt drawn to him.

Thad, with his white thatch of hair and his face as speckled as a turkey egg, with his cheerful disposition and lively ways, liked the quietness and the dark, handsome look of his new friend. Thad had never had boys or girls near his own age for friends, and Beau said he had two sisters at home. One was near Thad's own age, which was twelve, and the other was nine.

"You couldn't keep me away," he said in answer to Beau's invitation. "I'll be right proud to see your sisters."

The surest way to get anywhere in those days was on horseback, unless you liked walking, which nobody did. Everybody rode a horse, even women like Louisa Conway. She had been riding all her life and could sit a horse as well as any man.

Louisa Conway and Ellie Clark kept urging their husbands to take a day off for a visit with the Bransons, but the men kept putting them off. Thad was as anxious as the womenfolk to make the trip. Finally Mrs. Conway said, "Sampson, a week from today Ellie Clark and I are going to spend the day with Mrs. Branson. If you menfolk want to go along with us, I reckon you'll be welcome. If not, then we'll get along with what protection Thad can give us."

Thad was sure then that they were going, for when his mother called his father Sampson, he knew her mind was made up. Father knew it, too. It was not really as bad as mother Conway made it sound, for both she and Ellie Clark were as expert with a gun as any man or boy in the country.

So it was that as one spring morning dawned, when the redbirds, the mockingbirds, and the gentle-voiced bluebirds were trying out their first songs of the day, Mrs. Ellie Clark (whom Thad always called "Mis' Ellie," according to Southern custom), joined Thad and his mother at the Conway gate. Ellie was riding a tough little buckskin pony that had a black stripe from mane to tail. In front of Ellie was a little boy, and another one rode behind her.

Ma rode Travis's Blue Hornet, a strong, active horse that could smell an Indian as far away as any dog. Thad was on Little-bit, who would also warn of Indians, when they started down the creek trail that the cattle had made.

They traveled in a southward direction across rolling prairie, with dim blue rimrocks and ridges in the distance. The air was sweet with the heady perfume of buffalo clover, known today as bluebonnets, which for miles on end turned the earth into a reflection of the blue sky. On some slopes were acres of gold, where coreopsis blooms waved on their tall stems. It was a wide and seemingly empty land. To Thad it was full of wonders and surprises.

When the sun rose high, it beat on the heads of the riders,

who were glad when the path dipped into the cool, tree-shaded depths of the creek. At last they sighted a cluster of wagons at a bend in the creek, and saw the scattered herds of the Branson spread.

Mrs. Branson was expecting them, for Ben Atkins and Travis had been down this way a few days before and told her of mother Conway's plans.

"M-m-m, victuals!" Thad exclaimed when he caught the odor of food cooking on the outdoor fire.

A middle-aged, plump black woman tended the cooking. She was Aunt Dulcie, wife of Uncle Wash. Both of them worked for the Branson family. Thad had seen Uncle Wash once when he was riding after cattle with the men.

"Breakfast was a long time ago," Thad remarked as they approached, "and I'm starving." Twelve miles of riding had given him an appetite.

"You'll have to wait at least three hours, Thad," his mother reminded him. "It isn't more than nine o'clock now."

"We're still living in the wagons," Mrs. Branson apologized, but she pointed to where the men had laid a foundation for a house and had a rock chimney half built.

Marcella Branson was a small, friendly woman with dark, flashing eyes. Her crisp, wavy hair was drawn into a knot at the back of her neck. She talked softly but rapidly with a smooth-flowing accent that Thad had never heard before. Later he learned why her speech was different from that of Ben Atkins, although both of them were from Kentucky. Mrs. Branson had been a schoolteacher before she was married, and was careful of her English. Most of the people of central Texas in that day were not. Thad noticed that the white collar of her blue dress was fastened with a cameo pin. The letter M was worked into the wrought gold of its lower edge.

Besides Beau, there was another boy, three-year-old Stevie, with golden hair and his mother's bright brown eyes. He seemed to be the pet of the whole family, especially of his older sister and of Aunt Dulcie.

To Thad, the most attractive members of the family were Melissa and Cecilia. "Lissy" and "Celie," they were called. Two prettier little girls Thad had never seen before, and, he thought, never would he see any so pretty again. His experience with girls was admittedly scant, for besides the Morton girls, several years older than he, who lived fifteen miles northeast on Lonesome Creek, and some cousins he had met on a trip to Fort Worth, he had never known any girls.

Thad was only a rough frontier ranch boy, but he loved anything pretty. He could scarcely take his eyes from these two little girls—Melissa with her dark, curling hair and intensely blue eyes, and Cecilia, with hair the color of honey in a clear glass and dark, red-brown eyes. They were dressed alike except that Celie wore a pink-and-white-striped dress while Lissy's was blue and white.

"Come on down to the creek and I'll show you something," Beau invited. But before they started, Melissa brought some cookies for them.

"Aunt Dulcie says these will stay our stomachs until dinnertime," she said. Thad was sure they would not spoil his dinner, so, munching cookies, he followed the three others toward the sheds their father had built a little way from the creek bank.

They went down a little trail through a thick growth of sumac until they reached the creek bed, where tall trees grew between high banks. There was a dark pool of water where the spring floods had washed a hole at a bend in the creek. A giant cottonwood tree leaned out over the pool, keeping it in deep shade. On the opposite bank other old trees leaned across and mingled their branches with those that reached out to meet them.

It was a dark and mysterious place. Thad thought it would be a wonderful spot for a boy to have a secret hideaway, and that is just what Beau Branson and his sisters had made there. When Thad was led through the thick underbrush, he saw a faint trail on the bank above the pool. Beau lifted a screen of wild plum and sumac bushes and revealed the mouth of a cave.

They went inside. Beau dropped the screening branches, and it was almost as dark as a cellar. No one would have suspected the existence of such a cave, so perfectly was it hidden from public view.

There was a shelf dug from the wall of the cave on one side. Some candles were there, and Beau lighted one. On the shelf also was a row of tin boxes that caught Thad's eye.

"What are those?" he asked.

"That's our kitchen safe," Melissa explained. "Beau lets us play here, too, and this is our fort. When we play Indians we come in here to hide from them."

"What have you got in the safe?" Thad asked.

Melissa opened the boxes one by one. In the first was some jerky, or dried beef. It would keep for a long time if it did not get damp. In another there were some dry biscuits and corn bread. In one there was a handful of dried peaches and some dried apples. In the last there were several cookies. Melissa was still carrying two of the cookies she had brought from the wagons, and Celie had one. These they put into the cooky box and took out some of the older ones which were no longer very soft.

"I put these in here last week. We'll eat them now and save our new cookies for the next time we come," Melissa explained.

Thad laughed. "I never saw such little squirrels for hoarding victuals," he said.

They stayed and played at Indians and settlers until they heard Mrs. Branson calling them to dinner. Thad had never had so much real fun.

Thad did full justice to the dinner. Afterward Melissa, who seemed to be something of a tomboy in spite of her dainty appearance, said, "Come on. Let's show Thad the bobwhite's nest."

A little way from the wagons, beneath a bush, was the bobwhite's nest they wanted to show Thad. When Thad saw the eighteen eggs in it he was thrilled.

"Mustn't touch them," Melissa warned him, "or the mother won't come back."

"I know," he said. "I've got one near our house that I'm watching, but there are only twelve eggs in it. I'm fixing to get me a couple of pet bobwhites from the bunch."

"How are you going to catch them?" Beau wanted to know. Thad knew then that Beau had not lived in the country very long or he would not have needed to ask such a question.

"Just before they hatch I'm going to put some of them under our old setting hen and let her finish hatching them."

Thad had to leave for home then, for his mother was calling. It had been one of the happiest days of his life. He had never realized until now that he was lonely or that he needed the friendship of other boys and girls.

As he rode toward home with his mother and Mis' Ellie, Thad lagged behind, thinking about the Bransons. Girls, he decided, were something special. They were not rough like boys. They were pretty and gentle in their ways—at least the Branson girls were. He made up his mind that if they did not come to visit soon he would make an opportunity to go down and see them again. His mother could not get away very often, but his father or some of the men would be riding that way now and then looking after the cattle. His father was shorthanded because of the war, so even Thad had to spend hours in the saddle helping with the work. He would try to manage it so that he would be along the next time any of the men had to ride south toward the Bransons'.

They had gone perhaps six miles along the home trail when suddenly Little-bit pricked up her ears, snorted, and began pulling at the bit. She showed every sign of wanting to get away from that neighborhood fast. Thad knew the signs. He put his spurs to her and caught up with his mother and Mis' Ellie.

"Ma, there's Indians! Little-bit says they are somewhere close. She smells them!"

Blue Hornet was acting the same way now, and mother said, "Here, Ellie, give me one of those young ones." She stopped her horse, reached over and took little Tommy Clark, and set him in front of her on the saddle.

Then a faraway dull thumping sound reached Thad's ears. Indian drums! His ears were as sharp as a coyote's. The women had not heard the sound.

Spotted Boy and the Comanches

"Ma, don't you hear those drums?"

"I do!" Mis' Ellie cried. "Indian drums!" Mother Conway listened for a second. Then she heard it—the rhythmic thumping of distant drums.

"Let's head for home fast!" she cried.

No one needed urging. Even the horses ran as fast as they could pump their legs.

The drums could mean only one thing. There was an Indian camp not far away, and the horses sensed the danger. Any frontier horse that had ever spent time in the hands of Comanches knew their cruelty and dreaded it.

An arrow zinged past Little-bit's head, letting them know they were being pursued. Dropping behind the women, Thad watched the trees along the creek and cocked his gun, a Colt's .45 his father always made him carry. Little-bit fought her bit to keep up with the others, but Thad held her back. A movement, no more than the flutter of a bird, it seemed, caught his eye. It was among the bushes at the edge of the timber. Thad shot toward it, then gave Little-bit her head. There were no more arrows. After a little they eased up on their pace. Ellie Clark's little ones had not let out a murmur. They were frontier babies.

Three miles from home they met father Conway and Ben Atkins coming to meet them.

"We got to worrying about you-all," father explained, "after Ben came in from down this way and said he heard Indian drums."

"Yes, we heard them, too," mother told him. "We hurried for a while after that."

"They shot at us, too," Mis' Ellie said, "but Thad scared them away."

His father looked at Thad approvingly. "Good for you, son," he said. "I reckon you'll do."

Thad squirmed with embarrassment. "Aw, it wasn't anything," he said.

"I suspect it was just a few young braves that chased us," mother said. "They were out to take some scalps and horses the easy way."

16

There was an Indian camp not far away, and the horses sensed the danger. Just then an arrow zinged past Little-bit's head.

"Well, you shouldn't go off by yourselves anymore," father told them. "Next time there might be more than a few young braves, and they'd get you. It isn't safe."

Mrs. Clark laughed quietly. "Living in this part of Texas isn't safe any way you look at it, Mr. Conway," she said. "But we won't be taking any more chances than we have to."

Father shook his head as he unsaddled in the lot. "I'm powerful afraid that we're in for a lot of Comanche raiding this summer," he said. "It's mighty early for them to be sneaking around so close to the settlements."

Comanche! Comanche!　　　3

FATHER Conway was different from some of the men of the Texas frontier. He was a devout believer in the Bible and governed all his dealings by what he believed it taught. Every evening at eight o'clock, just before they went to bed, he called the whole family together. His call included all who were at home and any of the cowhands who were of a mind to come for family prayers. Each evening, in reverent tones that impressed Thad's mind, he read a passage from the Bible. Then, while all present dropped to their knees, he offered a fervent prayer, and to Thad it seemed that pa knew God was listening. To close, they sang a hymn.

The thoughts of confidence expressed and the stately language of the Book stirred the boy's soul. The poetry in some passages thrilled him just as did the thunderstorms and the glowing beauty of autumn. It was the only literature Thad knew at that time, and it filled his thoughts with an awareness of the joy and beauty of creation.

Mother Conway had given him all the schooling he had had up to that time. Later they were to have a school four miles away on Fiddleneck Creek for about three months each year. Thad's memory was good, so, because his mother made him do it, he learned many of the texts father read in evening worship.

For the last ten days in July one year, a protracted meeting was held at the Conway Double Bar O Ranch. It was a sort of old-fashioned camp meeting. Brother Heston had come from Waco, and word had been passed to the ranchers for miles around of his coming.

The Conway men put up a brush arbor and made some pole benches which were not too uncomfortable when padded with quilts. They spread wild hay on the ground under the arbor, and so they had a meetinghouse.

Spotted Boy and the Comanches

Families came from far and near, on horseback and in wagons, prepared to camp out for a week. The menfolk wore guns in their belts, and every saddle boot held a rifle.

From early morning until evening there was preaching and singing. Thad got more out of the association with other boys and girls than he did from the preaching, but the singing satisfied a certain need he felt.

Father Conway remarked, "One thing sure. Everybody here is well nourished both physically and spiritually, what with the beefs we barbecue and all the fixin's the women make to go with the meat. Preacher Heston gives us the rest of it."

There was one thing the preacher said several times in his sermons that worried Thad. We must love all of God's children, he said. Did that mean Comanches? Thad wondered.

After one of these sermons Thad and Beau listened while a rancher, Lafe Allen, from twelve miles over on Blanket Creek, argued hotly with Preacher Heston outside the meetinghouse.

"Brother Heston, are you tellin' us we've got to love those sneakin', murderin' Comanches?"

Brother Heston answered quietly, "No, *I'm* not telling you that. It was Jesus Christ who said, 'Love your enemies, bless them that curse you, do good to them that hate you, and pray for them which despitefully use you, and persecute you.' "

Lafe Allen shook his head impatiently. "Well, I don't consider that a Comanche is human, and I could never find it in my heart to love one of the rascals." His sentiments were so like Thad's that the boy stood with other men and boys to listen to the argument.

"When you get acquainted with a person, any kind of person, when you know his troubles and share his joys and understand his way of thinking, then you can love him," the preacher pointed out.

Another rancher, Chet Owen, who had seen his son killed, his house burned, and his cattle stolen by Comanches, said bitterly, "A man would have to overlook a sight of evil in a Comanche to ever get to love him."

"No more, perhaps," Preacher Heston replied, "than the Lord has to overlook in each one of us in order to love us. And the only way I know to put an end to the hate between Indians and white men is for us who know the Lord to pray that both they and we will have His love in our hearts."

Thad did not hear the rest of the argument, for at that moment he saw Charlie Bynum driving the cows across the creek and into the lot.

"Come on, Beau," Thad said. "Time to milk and get the chores done."

The two boys ran to the kitchen, picked up the milking pails, and went to the lot. On the way Thad said, "I'm like Mr. Lafe Allen. I could never love a Comanche, and I *hate* the one who keeps stealing Little-bit."

Late one afternoon when there was no meeting in progress, Travis said, "Let's go coon hunting."

Beau and Thad ran for their shotguns, and Thad whistled up old Whizzer. Travis called his hunting hounds, Bugle and Lady Lou. They set off down the creek, following the dogs. The thought of Indians at that time of day never entered their minds.

They had gone perhaps three fourths of a mile down the creek, slipping through the bushes on the banks, when the dogs found the track of a coon. Thad knew it was a coon by the way Whizzer bayed, just as well as though he had told him in so many words. The dogs were in the creek bed between banks about fifteen feet high. They yelped excitedly, going farther down the creek. The boys hurried after them as fast as they could travel, dropping down into the bed of the creek where the going was easier.

There was only a small stream of water in the creek bed, but here and there at the roots of some tall old tree, a hole had been washed out by the spring floods, leaving a deep, dark pool of water.

They ran at least another quarter of a mile before they came upon the dogs. As they arrived, the coon started to climb the trunk of a tall pecan tree. Whizzer made one big leap and pulled him down. The dogs were on the coon, a big old fellow, in a flash.

21

Whizzer hung on for dear life. The coon tried to drown the dog, and came near doing it, too, for the boys could not get in a shot.

Fighting them off the best he could, the coon plunged into the water.

Whizzer hung on for dear life. Thad was not sure, in fact, that Whizzer could have turned loose if he had wanted to, for the coon had sunk his teeth into one dangling ear and was clawing with all four feet at his underside. The other dogs had wisely loosened their hold when the coon hit the water. The coon proceeded to try to drown old Whizzer, and he came near to doing it, too, for the boys could not get in a shot without risking hitting Whizzer. At the last moment Whizzer, struggling desperately, managed to get loose and ran howling to where Thad was standing.

At that moment Thad became aware of a prickly feeling at the back of his neck. Someone was looking at him from behind, he felt sure. He whirled around and there, on the high bank above, were three brown faces, two with remnants of war paint smeared on them. They had been watching the fight between Whizzer and the raccoon, and were laughing heartily.

Thad let out a yell. "Hey! Indians!"

The other boys looked and grabbed for their guns.

Of the three faces, one in particular was to remain in Thad's memory. The only Indians he had ever seen were a few friendly Tonkawa scouts, and the painted Comanches with whom he had fought now and then. They had shown evil-looking faces. This face was the face of a boy, unpainted, laughing at the dog-and-coon fight, and friendly looking. For a moment Thad could have liked him. The others disappeared the instant he had yelled "Indians!" But that one, still smiling, drew away more slowly.

All thought of the raccoon was forgotten. The boys were afoot a mile from home. Since the Indians were on top of the bluff, they had every advantage. The white boys had no idea how many Indians there were, but the Indians knew the boys' situation exactly.

Still they had been laughing, and they appeared to be no older than Travis and Beau and Thad. But how many more were there back in the woods on the creek bank? Whizzer now went sniffing after the Indians until Thad, fearful of what might happen to him, called him back.

The three boys waited where they were for half an hour, their backs to the broad trunk of an old pecan tree. But nothing happened. Finally Trav said, "Come on. Let's chance it. I think there were just those three boys."

Slipping along the creek bank from tree to tree, they reached home about dark with a story to tell. Indian appearances caused a lot of interest on the frontier and with good reason. There was hardly a family at the Conway ranch for the meeting that had not lost at least one member to Comanche raiders.

For a while after that the boys took more care about venturing away from home without older companions and without horses. For a while, that is.

*   *   *

Lev Buchanan from up on Windy Creek was at the meeting. He had brought his wife, Mis' Sally, and their twin grandsons, Timmy and Tommy. The twins' father, Buck Buchanan, and their mother, Mis' Laurie, were there, too, but the little boys were seldom seen apart from their grandmother. They were as alike as two peas from a pod. Anyone could see that they were the two most important people in Mis' Sally's life. The way they followed her about reminded Thad of a doe with twin fawns.

But to the young folk, Mis' Sally was the most interesting member of the family. Before she was old enough to remember, Mis' Sally had been stolen by Comanches. When she was about eight years old, she had been rescued by Rangers after a battle at Possum Springs. She could speak no tongue but Comanche when they found her.

"No one knew whose young one I was," she told the young folk. "I reckon all my family had been massacred at the time the Comanches stole me. So the Rangers gave me to a rancher, Mr. Bill Judson, and his wife to raise."

"How did you come to get married to Mr. Lev?" Beau asked.

"Oh, Lev Buchanan was a hand riding for pa Judson, and when

I was eighteen years old we just up and got married," she said. "That's all there was to it." Her eyes twinkled when she told them that, and they were pretty sure that had she chosen, she could have made quite a story of that.

Thad had never seen anyone who enjoyed singing as Mis' Sally did. As his father described it: "Mis' Sally hasn't got a mite of a tune in her, but her way of making music is to pat her foot and throw back her head and squall like a wounded bobcat."

Thad decided that was as good a description as one could give. Mis' Sally was skinny, with faded, straw-colored hair and wrinkled, sunburned skin. The children considered her an old woman, but she was probably not more than forty-five or fifty years of age.

Her husband Lev often said, "My wife uses a voice for talking that would do for calling the hogs."

Thad and his friends followed her around to listen to stories of her life with the Comanches. She would spit words from the Comanche language at them, and Thad was able to pick up some of their speech in that way.

"I'll tell you young ones," she would say, "Comanches are just people. Their ways suit them all right, but I like our ways better."

"But they steal children and treat them mean.," Cecilia said.

"They steal children, sure enough," Miss Sally replied, "but once they get them used to their ways they just try to make good Comanches of them. They teach them that Comanches are the good folks and white people the bad ones. 'Long Knives,' they call us."

"Were you glad when the Rangers rescued you?" Melissa asked.

"I'll say not. I fought them tooth and nail. I was all Comanche. That's all I knew. No, I am not afraid of the Comanches, not a bit. For myself, that is. But for these little ones, I do hope and pray that they'll never get hold of them. They'd make Comanches of them. I've seen it done time and time again."

For the first time in months Thad's older brothers, Reed and Giles, rode in. They were at home for several days of the meetings, but then they had to leave to join their companies of Rangers.

25

Spotted Boy and the Comanches

When the meetings were ended and the people began scattering toward their homes, Thad rode Little-bit alongside the Branson wagon for several miles. Then as it disappeared into the woods along the creek, he stopped on a little knoll and waved as long as he could see it. The girls and little Steve waved from the back of the wagon, and Beau waved his hat for a minute, then galloped after the wagon and out of sight.

*   *   *

As Thad was coming in one evening driving the four milk cows from the pasture on the other side of the creek, he heard an owl hoo-hooing softly in the creek bottom. Another answered from below in the woods. Little-bit cocked her ears at the sound, snorted, and pulled at the bit.

"You hear Indians, Little-bit?" he asked her. He had a queer crawly feeling when the calls came again. Even though they were a good imitation of an owl's hooting, he was sure they were Indian signals. He hurried the cows along as fast as he could to the milking lot, where he found Travis pitching wild-grass hay into the barn loft.

"There're Indians around, Trav," Thad announced.

Travis rumpled his brother's hair and laughed. "What makes you think there are Indians around, young'un?"

"Little-bit says so. Besides, there are owls hooting in the woods."

"Maybe they *are* owls," Trav argued, but Thad was sure Trav believed him.

"Huh-uh," Thad said. "It's too early in the evening for owls. Besides, Little-bit always knows when Indians are around."

"Better get the saddle horses into the corral and fasten the gate," Travis said.

When father and the hands, Charlie Bynum, Ben Atkins, and Tom Weaver, came in, they helped make everything as secure as possible.

At bedtime Trav and Thad stepped out onto the back porch to listen. There was no unusual sound. But when they were in their beds, Thad lay with his head in the window, so he could hear better.

After he had lain there a long time listening, he heard again the hoo-hooing of an owl and the answer. One call came from near the horse barn. Travis heard it, too. They got up and put on their breeches and boots. They took their guns in their hands and crept outside.

They walked around the house and after a long while went to the corrals. The cows were all in their lot, and in the horse corral only Little-bit and Blue Hornet seemed uneasy. The rest of the horses munched placidly.

"No Indians around now," Travis said. Thad was not so sure, but he followed him back to bed.

Before daylight the next morning, while the family was getting up and mother was in the kitchen starting breakfast, Joe Rivers from seven miles up on Windy Creek came pounding into the Conway yard on a winded horse.

"Mr. Conway," he said, "Indians have been raiding up our way. They ran off all my riding stock and killed old man Lev Buchanan and scalped him. They must have carried off Mis' Sally and those twin young ones of Buck's."

"What about Buck and Mis' Laurie?" mother wanted to know.

"They went to Waco a week ago and took the older children. They should be back any day now."

"Has anyone sent for the Rangers?" father asked.

"Yes, sir, we sent Charlie Gibson after them, but there's no telling how long it will be before they come."

"Little-bit and Blue Hornet were telling the truth after all," Travis said.

"Might as well get into our fighting gear and not wait for Rangers," father said. "We'll help run them down and try to get your horses back. But we can't help poor old Lev Buchanan."

"Come and get your breakfast before you go," mother said.

Thad was buckling on his gun belt, getting ready to go out and see about Little-bit and go along on the Indian hunt, when his mother said, "Now, Thad, you just get any notions about hunting Indians out of your head."

"Oh, pa!" he wailed. "Can't I go along? I'm as good a shot as any man on the place."

"Yes, son, you are that," his father agreed. "But you had better stay here and look after ma and the stock. Can't tell what we might run into, nor how long we'll be gone. Ben Atkins hurt his game leg when his horse rolled him yesterday, so he'll be here to help."

"But ma's as good a shot as any of us," Thad protested. "Why do I have to stay at home?"

"No whining now, Thad. Do as I say." Thad knew there was no use begging any more, so, keeping his gun belt on, he went out to do the before-breakfast chores—milking, watering, and feeding.

"Hiya, Little-bit," he called as he approached the lot gate. "You sure know your Indians. I reckon they were just passing us by last night."

There was no answering nicker. Little-bit was not in the corral nor in the barn. Neither were Blue Hornet or any of the rest of the riding stock. There were several moccasin tracks in the mud beside the watering trough. Little-bit and the other horses had been stolen by the raiding Comanches after all. Thad found where they had got them out of the corral. They had taken the fence apart pole by pole in one place and driven them through.

"Poor Little-bit!" he exclaimed aloud. "You hate those Comanches, and now they've got you again. They won't be good to you, either."

Thad called to his father, Travis, and Ben Atkins. The boy was still talking to the absent Little-bit as he walked around investigating the work of the Comanches when the three menfolk reached the corral.

"What are you talking to yourself about, young'un?" Travis asked jokingly. Tears were flowing down Thad's face, but they were tears of anger and of fear for Little-bit.

"Comanches, that's what! They got Little-bit."

His father was looking around the corral and barn.

"Looks like the mare will have company from home," he said.

28

A hoarse whinny from outside the fence attracted their attention. There was old Nick the mule with his head over the fence calling to them. An arrow was sticking in his thigh, and a broken rawhide rope dangled from his neck.

"Nick! You got away from them!" pa Conway said. "Might have known you would!"

If ever an animal was his own boss it was Nick, the big, raw-boned, long-legged mule. When it suited his fancy to stay in the lot with the other stock, he stayed. When he wanted to go somewhere else, he simply backed off to a far corner, bunched his long legs under his body, and made a run and a jump that took him sailing over the top fence rails.

But Nick was the smartest worker on the place. Father always said of him, "Nick seems to know just what it is you're trying to do when you work him, and he does his best to get it done right."

"How do you suppose he got away from those Indians?" Charlie Bynum wondered.

"I wouldn't put it past him to have bitten a chunk out of whatever Comanche was unlucky enough to try to hold him," Travis said.

Father laughed. "He'd be up to just such as that."

"I declare to my time!" Ben Atkins complained. "It's getting so a fellow can barely catch up a bronc and break him to where he can ride him, when along come some of those Comanche varmints and steal him. Now I'm afoot again after I've just spent three weeks breaking that old rope-tailed Nubbin to the saddle and lariat."

"Well, it looks as though none of us has a mount, outside of old Nick here, and he does his best work to the wagon or plow," Travis said.

"We'll have to use him," father said. "Saddle him up, Trav, and see if you can round up some horses from the range that they overlooked. We'll have to go after those murdering horse thieves. They might have Mis' Sally Buchanan and those little ones, if they haven't already killed them."

Spotted Boy and the Comanches

In an hour or two Travis came back driving eight or ten head of saddle horses ahead of him. The Comanches had not found them.

"They were holed up in a draw under a rimrock by that little creek. There's a lot of thick-growing willow and cottonwood along it," he said.

There were saddles enough to go around, and mother had some jerky and bread and dried-fruit fried pies packed for them by the time they were ready to travel. Thad watched them go while he drowned himself in self-pity. He was past twelve, and he thought they should have taken him along.

Thad and his mother shared the chores while Ben Atkins looked after the range stock. They got along all right for a couple of days. And then Thad's father came riding home. They were all ears to hear what had happened.

"We had a hard time finding the trail of the Comanches," he told them. "But when we finally struck it where several bands had joined and were heading west, I was so worn out that I had to turn back. I'm getting old, I reckon—too old to ride far and then fight Indians." He sank wearily into his chair beside the fireplace.

"I see you have some buffalo meat on your saddle, Mr. Conway," Ben Atkins said. He had unsaddled for father.

"Yesterday we struck a small bunch of buffalo," father said. "It looked like they had been hunted and were separated from the main herd. I just brought a few ribs and steaks home with me. The fellows needed most of it. They would be running short of rations pretty soon if we hadn't shot this meat. Men from all the ranches for forty or fifty miles up and down these creeks joined us. They'll put up a battle if they ever catch up with those murderers. They're all stirred up about what the Indians did to Lev Buchanan and his family."

"Tell us about it," mother asked him. "Did you see any of the Comanches?"

"No, we didn't run into any of them," father answered. "But as I told you, we followed their trail. They had a sight of horses with them, so it wasn't hard to follow. Some Rangers joined us near Lost

Springs, and they had a couple of Tonkawa scouts with them. But we saw plenty of the depredations the Indians had done." He shook his head sadly. "We found a lot of the Double Bar O cattle slaughtered. They took only the liver and the heart and a little of the meat from each one. They took the hides of some of them, too."

"I don't suppose we can blame them too much for wanting to make the white folk miserable when we are taking their country away from them," mother remarked. "But it's natural for our men to try to wipe them out, too."

"We could live with them peaceably like we do with the Tonkawas, Mis' Louisa," Ben Atkins said, "if they just would. There's plenty of room for all of us."

"There is if the Comanches would settle down in one place and work like we do," pa said. "The Comanches have been a plague to all the other tribes since time out of mind, and none of them has any love for a Comanche, though the Kiowas have joined them for their own self-protection at times."

Ten days after Father Conway returned, Thad walked, yawning, early one morning to the milking shed. He heard a low whicker, and there at the gate of the horse corral was Little-bit. She was waiting just as though she had never been away, though she was as disreputable looking as when he had first seen her. He could count her ribs, and she had a sore mouth and hobble-burned ankles. She seemed barely able to stand. He shouted for his father and mother to come, and then went to put his arms around the little mare's neck.

Father had told them that Reed and Giles were among the Rangers that had joined the ranchers to fight the Indians, and that when the trouble was over they would stop at home for a few days.

"I do hope that will be right soon," mother said. "I do miss them so!"

The Indians seemed to be always a day or two ahead of the white men. They would separate into small bands for a while and then join forces again at some distance. The country out there in western Texas was so vast and empty that hunting a band of Comanches was like looking for a pin in a strawstack. Besides, they had tricks of covering their tracks, such as driving the stock for a long way in water when they came to a stream, or following across a wide, flat country across loose rock and sand where the constant wind would soon wipe out their tracks.

However, early one morning the Rangers and cowmen surprised a small band of Comanches where they were camped around a water hole, and almost wiped them out. Those that survived ran away and left the horse herd. One of the white men, Paul Roland from the Turkey Peak country, was hurt quite seriously. The best result of the encounter was that they recaptured a lot of stolen horses, among them a sizable bunch of Double Bar O stock, both horses and mules. Blue Hornet was among them.

Shortly after, the Rangers were called to another part of the country that had suffered depredations. Now that the cowmen had so many of their horses and cattle to drive home, they returned to their ranches. The Conways learned all this from their sons, Travis, Reed, and Giles, and from Charlie Bynum.

Comanches Strike Again 4

THAT was a summer of Indian alarms and raids, and something besides. When Reed and Giles got home from chasing Indians, they were both burning with fever.

"It's that bad water you've been drinking out there on the plains," mother diagnosed their ailment. But this opinion changed a day or two later when both of them woke up with a bright-red rash that got worse as the day wore on.

"Measles!" mother then exclaimed. "Not one of you children has ever had the measles. Some of these new settlers have brought it into this country, I reckon. Now every last one of you will catch it."

Reed groaned. "I always heard measles was a youngster's disease; I never dreamed it could make a person feel as bad as I do."

Mother was not too sorry. She would have her boys at home for a while now. "It goes harder with grown folks than with young ones," she said.

The next thing, the rest of the family were down with it—Ben Atkins, then Travis, then Thad. Mother and father Conway had already had the disease, so were immune. So was Charlie Bynum. Thad had never been sick in his life, to speak of, and he felt he was making up for all the diseases he had missed.

They were all well enough to be up and sitting around when they had their worst attack from the Comanches. It came just before daylight. All the day before Little-bit and Blue Hornet had been nervous and fidgety. When Charlie brought in the cows from across the creek, he said, "Mr. Conway, I feel like there is something wrong."

"How's that?" Mr. Conway asked.

"Several things," Charlie said. "First, I heard a turtledove calling from over in the open country. That was on my left. It didn't sound much like a dove, either. Then suddenly, away over to my right at

When Charlie brought the cows from across the creek, he said, "I feel like there is something wrong." The horses had been nervous.

a good distance, several bobwhites flew up, a family of them. They had bedded down for the night. There wasn't any coyote or fox or anything I could see to scare them up."

"Is that all?"

"No, sir; old Whizzer here was trailing along behind me, and he growled and just kept a-growling and looking over toward where those bobwhites flew up."

"It doesn't sound too good, does it?" Mr. Conway said. "Better put someone on guard for the night."

When Reed heard about it, he sent a message to his company of Rangers who were camped about ten miles east of the ranch. All the saddle horses were tied between the house and the kitchen, which, on the Conway ranch as on many others, was separate from the living part of the house.

"Better bring your saddles inside the kitchen," Reed suggested. "We don't want to find ourselves afoot if the Comanches come."

Father Conway sat beside the fireplace with a rifle across his knee until midnight. Then Charlie Bynum took over until morning. None of them took off their clothes. No light was allowed.

It was still dark, and Thad was asleep, when Charlie gave the signal, "Everybody up! They're moving in on us!"

Thad pulled on his boots, which was all he had taken off, and tightened up the buckle of his gun belt and grabbed his hat. He reached the kitchen just as Reed and Giles came in. Travis came into the room a minute later. Ben Atkins had gone last night to summon the Rangers.

Outside the house a horse's shrill whinny told them there were strange horses about. But there was no answering call from beyond the creek.

"They've got their horses' noses pinched with those hackamore contraptions they make," Reed said. Thad knew what he meant. The Comanches had a way of braiding knots into their horses' hackamores just where, with a pull, the rider could pinch the nostril. It discouraged any horse from neighing or nickering. It was difficult enough for the horse to get his breath.

Spotted Boy and the Comanches

"They're out there, all right," Giles said. "It's a good thing we're all here. We can give them a stiff fight.

The Comanches had no doubt been watching the house for some time, getting ready to make an all-out attack on the Conway family. But the boys, Reed and Giles, had arrived at night, and almost everybody had been out of sight with the measles for several days. Consequently the Indians probably had no idea of the size of the family, or they would not have attacked.

It was at the time just before dawn when everything is gray and dim. One can imagine all sorts of things, but cannot be sure anything he sees is real. The Conways' house was built to resist assault. The shutters and doors were of thick oak planks, and the walls of the kitchen, which was the first part of the house pa had built, were of logs eighteen inches thick. The rest of the rooms, built on each side of a wide hall or breezeway, were of logs, too, though not such big ones as in the kitchen.

Loopholes had been made in every wall and in the shutters, so that those inside could see to fight back when the attack came. Each member of the family took up his station at one of these and waited. Ma sat ready to reload rifles and pistols for the others, but she also kept her own rifle at hand.

They did not have long to wait. A sudden shower of arrows came from the darkness, plus a few scattered rifle shots.

"They've been trading the cattle and horses they stole from us for those Mexican rifles," pa said sourly. "Now they use them on us."

Counting mother, who was as good a shot as any of the others, and Charlie Bynum and Bill Weaver, there were eight rifles.

"They're trying to set the roof afire!" Travis yelled from the front room. "They're shooting burning arrows!"

Father laughed softly. "Won't do them any good," he said. The roof was covered with wooden shakes, but underneath them was a thick layer of earth like that on the brush arbors the Mexicans built.

The members of the family were firing at the dim forms they saw now and again, but they were not able to tell whether they were scoring hits, and they could not estimate the number of Comanches. The Indians' yells, like the howling of coyotes, would lead one to think there were a dozen when there were only one or two. But there were more than a dozen Comanches out there; the Conways were sure of that. But whether there were twenty-five or a hundred, no one could say.

The Comanches must have been surprised at the force and accuracy of the return fire. Certainly they had not expected to find so many at the house. Then suddenly the attack ceased.

"They're still out there," Reed said with confidence. "And they'll be back. They're mounting their ponies."

He was right. After a little while there was a savage screaming and yelling. It seemed to Thad as though it would freeze the blood in his veins. It was the famous Comanche yell, the most blood-curdling set of noises human throats can make. It was meant to do just what it did do—scare the wits out of any poor soul who must listen to it.

Thad's heart seemed to be standing still. But his older brothers, who had fought many a battle with the Comanches, and father, who had fought them all his life, batted not an eyelid. They poured a hail of lead into the stream of warriors, now more easy to see in the early morning light, as they charged the house, yelling, screaming, shooting.

"They're a-horseback now," Giles commented. "This is their real try. If we can hold them now, we've got them licked."

The lead of the defenders must have had some effect, for the yells of the Indians died as they circled away from the house to get ready for a new attack and to pick up their dead and wounded.

An arrow had skimmed through a loophole in a window shutter and nicked Travis's shoulder. It bled some, but mother applied a bandage filled with soot from the fireplace to stanch the flow. Travis was now back at his post at the loophole, his rifle popping along with the others.

"Giles, you, Travis, and Charlie come with me. We'll get our horses and go after those devils," Reed suggested. "They're after our horses. We'll have to run them off or they'll get every one of them."

They had hardly saddled and mounted their horses when the Comanches renewed their attack. But at the same time from east of the house came a Comanche yell from many voices. Undoubtedly a large force was approaching from that direction, and Thad was stiff with fright. Their doom was sealed, he was certain.

Suddenly Reed started waving his hat and yelling like a Comanche himself. "There they come!" he hollered. "Those are my Rangers! Now run, you Comanches, run!"

The Comanches did not need to be told the battle was over. They faded from the scene as suddenly as they had appeared. The men followed them for a little way, then came back to the house and made preparations for an expedition against the raiders.

Reed's sergeant told Giles, "Your company will be along in a few hours, captain. We sent word to them. They were over on Blanket Creek, and it shouldn't take them long to get here. It is only twelve miles."

"I'll wait for them, then," Giles said.

"We'd better give those Comanches a good lesson while we're at it," muttered Reed. "Drive them out of this part of the country and try to get some of the ranchers' stock back, and maybe some captives. Yellow Cloud and his band will never give us peace until we do."

Mother was getting breakfast for the men of the family, with Thad helping her. The Rangers had fires going in the yard to cook their own meal. After eating, the men, leaving only father, Ben Atkins, and Thad behind, set out on their expedition. Even Travis went along. Giles stayed to wait for his Rangers to come.

After the excitement those at home went about their chores as usual. Giles helped Thad with the milking, and Ben Atkins fed the stock. What would surely have been a massacre at the Conway Double Bar O Ranch had the older sons not been at home with the measles turned into a defeat for the Comanches. Besides, the quick follow-up by the Rangers might prevent further trouble from the Indians, and save some lives. No one was more anxious to put an end to the stealing and killing than father Conway.

"I've been fighting Indians all my life," he remarked, "from the Brazos to the Colorado, and my pa before me. I'm getting tired of it."

At ten o'clock that morning Giles's company of Rangers rode in, ready to join the pursuing party, the family supposed. But they brought news that changed these plans for the present. Giles stood and talked with his sergeant for some time before coming to the house.

"I've got bad news for you-all, mighty bad news," he said. "A band of Comanches attacked the Branson ranch this morning at daylight and massacred most of the family."

Mother was the first to get her breath after that announcement. Thad seemed to have no feeling. He could not take in the full meaning of Giles's words.

"All of them killed?" mother asked.

"The men don't know how many for sure," Giles said. "One of the Branson cowhands caught up with my men on their way here and told them. Ma, you better fix to come with us. We'll see what we can do, then we'll ride after the murderers."

"It was probably a bunch split off from the ones that attacked us," pa said.

"I reckon so," Giles agreed. "That's the way they work. I think all these are from Yellow Cloud's band. They hole up way out west, a hundred, maybe three hundred miles from here. Move around a lot so we can't pin them down. The country is so big and wild it is hard to find even a big band if they don't want to be found. They know we're coming almost as soon as we know it ourselves, and they scatter into small bands."

"Well, I've often wondered," mother remarked, "why, when a band makes a raid, our men can hardly ever find them."

Johnny Ainsworth, Giles's Ranger scout, said, "We can find Comanches out there sometimes, but try pinning down the band and the chief that's responsible for the raids. We just can't do it."

Spotted Boy and the Comanches

"I don't see why you can't, Mr. Johnny," Thad argued. "Don't the horses have the rancher's brands on them?"

"The horses are traded over into New Mexico and the branded cattle are either driven into Chihuahua or slaughtered by the time we find the guilty parties. When we do run onto them, they are just a band of innocent, hardworking Indians tending their own business."

"One-Eye" Johnny Ainsworth rode beside Thad on the way to the Branson ranch. Thad had met the scout many times and listened to his tales. Johnny could tell some that would put a boy's hair on end, too. When he was a boy of eight, his whole family had been killed by Comanches. He had managed to hide in the tall weeds, and they had overlooked him in the darkness. A neighbor had found him the next day and had raised him as his own.

As a boy he had been dedicated to the task of fighting Indians, and as soon as he was old enough he began working as a scout with the soldiers and Rangers. He had learned the Comanche language from captives and from scouts of other tribes. He had been captured by Comanches once and had been tortured before he could escape. The left side of his face was scarred and one eye had been put out. He wore a black patch over the eye so that he had a sinister look until he spoke or smiled. Actually he was a quiet, kindhearted man.

As they rode toward the Bransons' that day, he told Thad how he came to be scarred, and how his parents had been killed by the Comanches. Thad said, "I reckon you purely hate those Comanches, don't you, Johnny?"

He was surprised when Ainsworth shook his head. "Maybe I ought to, Thad," he said. "But I can't seem to hate anybody. It wears me out even not to like anyone. Those Comanches are living their lives like they have been raised to live. All I want is to help get them under control so that they can be taught a better way. Then we can all live together peaceably."

Thad could hardly believe the scout really meant what he was saying. "But, Mr. Johnny, I always heard—"

40

Mr. Johnny grinned at the boy. "You always heard that I am a Comanche killer, didn't you?"

Thad was embarrassed, but he nodded.

"Well, that's hardly the fact, Thad," Mr. Johnny said. "I've scouted for the soldiers and the Rangers because I speak the Comanches' language as well as any brave, and I've been the go-between in some of their talks and treaties. But I found out a long time ago that if I let myself hate them I would be no better than a Comanche."

"But they hate us!" Thad exclaimed.

"Yes, mostly they do, and sometimes it is with good reason, Thad. We Long Knives have not always acted like Christians in our dealings with them. They hate white folk, so they kill and torture them, men, women, and little children. If I would let myself feel like that toward them, I'd be as cruel and mean to them as they are to us. But I don't want to be like that."

Thad thought over Mr. Johnny's words as they rode on. He still believed he could really hate anyone who had harmed those pretty little girls, Celie and Lissy. His heart was heavy with dread. He wondered what had happened to Stevie. How could even a Comanche harm a sweet little boy like Stevie Branson?

Mr. Branson had finished his house, at least enough so that they had been living in it several months, but now it was a shambles. At first it appeared that no one was about, but as they went in at the front where the door had been broken and partly burned, they saw a form on the bed with a quilt drawn over it. Strangely, Thad would always carry in his memory even the pattern of the quilt. It was a Rose of Sharon design such as he had seen on his mother's and Mis' Ellie's beds. It was made with pretty pink and green and white pieces.

Wiley Branson sat on a broken chair beside the bed, his head in his hands. He looked up when father and mother Conway stood beside him. He motioned to the figure on the bed. "Marcella." That was all he said.

"Where are the rest, Wiley?" father asked.

41

Spotted Boy and the Comanches

Just then Clem Howard, one of Wiley Branson's cowhands, came in from the back. "Come on out here, and I'll tell you about it, Mr. Conway," he said, leading them toward the door. He nodded his head toward Wiley Branson, who had dropped his head in his hands again.

"Before daybreak," Clem began, "I heard the dogs barking. They made a terrible racket. I jumped up and put on my breeches and my boots and grabbed my gun belt. Wiley had heard them, too, and he was in the kitchen when I got there. The other hands, Jed, Solly, and Bart, had all gone yesterday to round up some cows with little calves on the far side of Blue Mountain. They won't be back for several days."

"You two didn't go out when the dogs barked, did you?" father asked.

"Yes, Mr. Conway, we did. I told Wiley that that was an old Indian trick. One or two Indians would get the dogs excited and then toll the menfolk away from the house while the rest of them did what they wanted to do at the house. That way they divided the strength of the family."

"And he wouldn't listen to you?" father asked.

"No, sir, he wouldn't. He said, 'Clem, you come with me. There are Indians out there in the pasture trying to run off our horses.' So I couldn't do anything but go along. I kept looking back at the house, but I didn't see anything, and pretty soon we were out beyond the barns, where the dogs were barking."

"Did you see any Indians?" father asked, as though he knew the answer already.

"Yes, sir, we did. Two of them. Young bucks they were, though we couldn't see them very well. They were at the foot of a tree with sticks in their hands tantalizing those dogs. I knew right then it was a trick and that it had worked. We had been away from the house for at least ten minutes. I yelled, 'Mr. Branson, they've tricked us. Look there!' The flames were rising in the direction of the house. We ran back as fast as we could go, and this is what we found." Clem spread his hands at the destruction around them.

"I see you put the fire out before it burned the whole house," father said.

"Yes, sir, that was the first thing we did. It hadn't got much of a start on the house. It was mostly the kitchen, and it is pretty much of a wreck."

Mother Conway began trying to straighten things out, but there was no place to begin, for the whole house was in a state of confusion. Boxes were hacked open, and their contents torn and scattered and most of them taken. The bureau drawers were empty on the floor. The Comanches loved to strut around in white folks' clothes, especially women's dresses.

Books and papers were torn and scattered as by a storm. In the kitchen, what was left of it, two bodies lay covered. Thad's mother would not let him look at them. "They are Wash and Dulcie," Clem informed them.

As they stood there, a groan came from one. Mother pulled away the quilt. Dulcie groaned again, then sat up, clutching at her head. Father and Clem carried her to a bed, and mother began sponging her face.

Thad started aimlessly poking around here and there inside and outside the house. He was hoping he could piece together for his own satisfaction what had become of the girls and Beau and Stevie, for they had not been seen since the attack.

On the ground outside the window of the room where Beau and Stevie always slept, he found the stuffed rag horse that had been Stevie's inseparable companion. Had they dragged him out of this window to his death? He stood and held the toy horse in his hand, wondering where Stevie was and whether he was still alive.

"I don't care what Johnny Ainsworth says," Thad said to himself. "I *hate* those Comanches. I purely hate them, and I'll kill every one of them I can get my hands on!"

Thad's captors were three young Comanche braves.

Capture!

5

"**P**OOR little smudged and torn rag horse! Where is the small boy with the laughing eyes who loved you?" · These were Thad's thoughts as he stood holding the little toy horse and praying that Stevie might still be found alive.

There outside the house by the chimney, he began to settle his thoughts. The grown-up folk would be working along one line to find out what had become of the girls and Beau and Stevie. Thad's thoughts took a different turn. He began to ask himself, "What would I have done if I had been in Beau's place and the Comanches had attacked?"

Beau always slept with Stevie, and he was devoted to his little brother. "Why, of course, I would try to save him, and the window would be the way out of the house that I would take!"

Just at that moment his thoughts were interrupted by One-Eye Johnny Ainsworth, who came running around the corner of the house. He stopped when he saw Thad.

"We're taking off to see if we can trail those Indians, Thad. Are you coming with us?"

Thad was afraid that if he asked pa for permission, he would tell him that he could not go. So he ran along with Mr. Johnny and got on Little-bit. Giles and ten of his company of Rangers were gathered to start.

"We'll scout out and see if we can strike their trail," Giles said. When he saw Thad, he asked, "Did pa say you could go along?"

Thad did not answer, so Giles added, "Come on. We'll be coming back pretty soon if we don't find their trail in this direction. If we do find it, you'll have to turn back right soon, because we can't have any young ones along on an Indian fight."

They struck the trail of the Comanches a little way beyond the creek crossing. The Indians had been driving a large herd of horses, almost all Mr. Branson owned. There were at least fifty head. The trail was not hard to follow. The white men could make faster time than the Indians could, so Giles figured that if they overtook the Indians and they proved too many for his men, he could send Thad back for the others.

They had not been riding for more than an hour when suddenly Mr. Johnny Ainsworth, who was scouting ahead, came back riding hard. "I've found the little one, Celie, killed by the Indians," he called.

Thad wanted with all his heart to go along and fight those Comanches. He felt sure he was old enough and smart enough to make a good Indian fighter. But he knew he had to obey orders and return home. He thought of what Mr. Johnny had said about not hating even Comanches, and wondered how Johnny could feel as he did. He wondered if he, Thad, could ever come to say that he did not really hate them. At that moment he hated every one of them with all his heart, in spite of what Preacher Heston had read from the Good Book about loving our enemies. That, he was certain, he could never do.

Mr. Branson seemed, from the time Clem and Thad had come back to the house, to lose hope for any of his family. Mother Conway tried to reassure him.

"You can never tell," she said, "what a Comanche will do. They are as liable as not to treat Lissy and the boys like their own children."

Mr. Branson considered it his own fault that he had lost his family. If he had known Comanche ways better, he would never have been lured away from the house by the barking of the dogs. The thought was about to drive him out of his mind.

Thad picked up the little stuffed horse again and started on the train of thought that had been interrupted. He still hoped that maybe Beau had done the thing Thad believed he would have done in the circumstances. By now it was late in the afternoon, and the sun was pouring in a golden flood through the western windows as he sat in the bedroom with the toy horse in his hand. He kept thinking of that day last spring when he had first come with mother and Mis' Ellie Clark to visit the Bransons. All the things they had done that day ran through his mind, until he thought of the cave in the creek bank that the children had called their fort.

His thoughts stopped right there. That was it! That was where he would have gone to hide from the Comanches! It was worth looking into.

"Ma," he called, "I'm going down on the creek for a while. I'll be back directly."

"All right, son," she answered him. "Don't be gone long. It will soon be dark."

Thad could not get there fast enough. He ran until he was out of breath. He crept along the slippery bank over the dark pool in the creek bed. He lifted the curtain of wild plum and sumac bushes gingerly. The back of his neck ran with prickles. Everything seemed as still as death. It was dark inside, and as he stood with the last of the branches in his hand, holding them aside, a voice hailed him from the dark.

"Thad Conway, it's you! I was afraid those Indians had found us." Another voice piped up gleefully before Thad could answer.

"T'ad, T'ad, we hide!" It was Stevie, rumpled, dirty little Stevie, still in his nightgown, but alive and well. He spied the small horse that Thad held in his hand, and ran to snatch it from his hand.

"Horsie, Stevie's horsie!" and he laughed gaily as though it had all been a happy adventure, running away in the night with big brother Beau and hiding to play Indians. They had eaten the food stored in the tin boxes and had drunk from a bottle of water the children always kept for their fort's water supply.

"Why did you stay down here so long?" Thad asked Beau. "The Comanches have been gone since morning."

"I was afraid to come out. I didn't know whether they had left or not at first. Later I was afraid to see what I would find. I was just about to come out and see how things were."

"How did you happen to come here in the first place?" Thad asked.

Spotted Boy and the Comanches

"When the Comanches first came, after Clem and pa had gone to see why the dogs were barking," he told Thad, "my first thought was what they would do to Stevie, so I yanked him from his bed and carried him through the window. I knew this was the safest place on the ranch, and for the time being, at least, the Indians were on the other side of the house. So I headed straight for this cave."

One of the hardest things Thad ever had to do was to tell Beau what awaited him at the house. Beau was stunned with grief and Thad tried to comfort him. "At least you have your pa and Stevie," he reminded him.

"But there are only the menfolk of our family left," he mourned.

Wiley Branson and Aunt Dulcie shouted with joy when Thad and the two boys walked in, and for a moment they seemed to think Melissa must be with them, too. Dulcie cried wildly and clasped Stevie to her ample bosom, rocking back and forth on the bed and crooning a soft tune to him.

"My baby! My baby!" she sang over and over. "My baby boy come back to Dulcie!"

Finding Beau and Stevie gave Mr. Branson new hope. "At least," he said, "I won't go sorrowing over *all* of my loved ones for the rest of my life."

Poor old Aunt Dulcie had a terrible blow on the head and several gashes on her body. She moaned constantly, both because of her physical pain and from sorrow at losing her husband. Mother and Mis' Ellie had their hands full looking after her.

Thad went with his father to their ranch the next day after they had buried the dead. They brought back a light buckboard with a couple of driving mules hitched to it to bring Aunt Dulcie home where mother Conway could care for her. Stevie went home with them, too. They had found a few of his clothes, but none of Beau's or Mr. Branson's, and only a few belonging to the girls and Mrs. Branson. The Comanches had either burned or stolen all the others.

"If Dulcie gets well," mother said, "she can stay with us and look after Stephen." Beau and his father also went home with the

Conways, but later Wiley went to work with the Rangers, who were searching for the Indians who had broken up his family.

Three or four weeks passed before the searchers came home again. They brought a haunch of buffalo meat, but that was all.

"We found out for sure that it was Yellow Cloud's band; they split up and hit both the Branson place and ours," Giles said.

"How did you learn that?" His father was skeptical.

"Some Tonkawa hunters we met had run across their trail out on the prairie west of here and followed them until they had come together again. They know Yellow Cloud well."

"Couldn't you find them, then?"

"By the time we got to where the Tonkawas had seen them, Yellow Cloud and his band were gone—no telling where. Maybe into Indian Territory where they will be safe, maybe into Mexico, where they'll also be safe. There was no trail we could follow after we got about seventy-five miles west of here."

"We're not giving up yet," Reed said. "We're going to get some scouts from the Tonkawas and some more Rangers."

"I'm going to make it my personal business to find Melissa or learn what has become of her," Wiley Branson said. "I hope you-all will look after my other two and Dulcie. My hands, Clem, Jed, and Sollie, will look after my cattle."

"They can all stay here with us, and welcome," said mother Conway.

For the rest of the summer Thad's thoughts were constantly on Melissa Branson. Where was she, and was she alive? If so, how were the Indians treating her? Sometimes he felt he could not bear not knowing. The thought of what had happened to little Celie and her mother haunted his dreams, but that was over and nothing could be done about it. Melissa, he hoped, was still alive. It was hard for him to know what to wish for her.

Beau Branson was seldom at the Conway home, for he spent most of his time with his father's cowhands looking after their cattle. But Stevie, with his happy, innocent ways, brought a great deal of pleasure to the Conway family. He loved Dulcie, who had been his nurse all his life, and since he could not understand the tragedy that had come to him, he was happy. Dulcie, who was rapidly recovering from her wounds, would not let him out of her sight.

"He's all I got left of my family," she would say. "Ain't nobody goin' to hurt him, 'ceptin' over Dulcie's dead body."

*   *   *

A boy of the Texas frontier in those days learned to ride a horse even before he could remember, and he would no more have left the house without a lariat coiled on his saddle and his gun in its holster than he would have started out without breeches. Thad had spent every spare minute of his life working with his rawhide lariat, twirling it in fancy loops, settling it around the neck of some unfortunate dog or calf or colt. Later on it was the range horses and cows that he practiced on. He also practiced shooting every day, either in search of meat for the family, such as antelope, deer, turkey, or quail, or on targets thrown into the air for him. This was no idle play, for handling a rope and shooting straight were necessary skills of a cattleman's daily work. Thad had become expert with rope and gun.

Now he was in dead earnest when he did his practicing. He had it in his mind that when spring should come he would go on his own search for Melissa Branson. It was only a hazy notion, and he had worked out no details of his plan. But he believed that somehow he would be able to help rescue her, if she was still alive, by being the best shot and the best hand with a rope that he could make of himself. But he never had a chance to try out his rescue plan.

One day in late October Thad and his brother Travis went up the creek about two miles to round up some cows with half-grown calves that their father wanted them to bring in to feed for the winter. Trav was doing a little wild-turkey hunting on the side.

Thad was riding Little-bit. It took only an hour or two to round up the cattle and head them toward home. But he had noticed as they rode up the creek that there were many large, thin-shelled pecans here—more than around the home place. He decided to gather some of these finer nuts to take home. Thad had something of the nature of a squirrel; he loved to gather wild produce in season. For that purpose he generally carried a bag strapped to the cantle of his saddle for gathering whatever he could find. By this time Travis had shot two wild turkeys and had tied them to his saddle.

"Trav," Thad said, "how about starting on home with the cows without me?"

"What have you got up your sleeve, young'un?" his brother wanted to know.

"I'd like to pick up some of those big pecans. There are a lot of them under these trees," Thad replied.

"Sure, run along, Thad; but don't go too far. I can travel pretty fast with these cows, and I don't want to have to holler you in."

It was now so late in the fall that they felt sure the Comanches had gone away for the winter. Therefore the boys felt fairly safe. But Thad in later years was to wonder at the chances they so often took. As soon as a Comanche raid was over and a chase made, the frontiersmen prowled about alone as though there was nothing in the world to fear.

Thad tied Little-bit to a tree on the high bank. Because his pistol and belt hampered him in stooping to pick up the pecans, he unbuckled the belt and threw it with the gun across Little-bit's saddle. Going down into the sandy bed of the creek under its canopy of tall pecan and cottonwood trees, he began to fill his sack with the pecans that lay thick beneath some of the trees.

A few nights before there had been a heavy frost that had opened the hulls and brought the ripe nuts down in a hurry. Now and then Thad could hear the pop of a late-falling nut as it rattled fifty feet or more and hit the gravel of the creek bed.

As he stooped to gather the nuts, Thad heard a slight sound that he knew was not made by any nut dropping.

A chill came over him, for he realized that by now Travis and the cows would be too far away for him to catch up with them

51

quickly. Even Little-bit was a good way from him, for he had worked farther up the creek as he gathered pecans. She was grazing on the mesquite grass on the high bank of the creek, downstream from Thad.

The feeling of chilliness had nothing to do with the weather. It grew on him as he stooped to pick up his half-filled bag of pecans, and he intended to start back to where he had left Little-bit. As he climbed from the green twilight of the heavily shadowed creek, he heard Little-bit snort with fright. Then he started to run. At the same moment a scent filled his nostrils, an odor made up of smoke and grease, horse, and oily skin—Indian smell!

He caught the sound of quiet-running steps behind him. Then he was seized from the back around the neck. A brown arm was under his chin, and two dark hands pinned his arms to his sides. One Indian had seized him from behind, while another had him in front. It was impossible for him to jerk loose.

He kicked and bit and screamed with rage and fright. He heard Little-bit squeal, and then he could hear her hoofbeats going away from him. He had left her tied, so someone must be riding her.

Hoping against hope that Travis could hear him, Thad yelled as loudly as he could: "Trav, Injuns! Run for your life! They've got me!" But he knew that Travis was too far away. A firm hand clasped his mouth and smothered his cries. He sank his teeth into the hand and received for his pains a sharp slap on the face that rocked his head on his neck. A whack over the head with a stick from the other Indian brought the blood streaming down his forehead and face and sent his brain spinning.

They pushed him along among the timber and across the stream in the bed of the creek. Half dazed, he stumbled now and then, and each time received a kick, or a blow on his back or head. He felt as though he were half dead when he was finally pulled up the opposite bank half a mile upstream from where he had been captured. He was tight and frozen inside, and his legs would scarcely bear him up. Here they stopped, and were joined by a band of eight more Comanche braves. Thad now took the opportunity to inspect his captors. Heretofore he had only had the impression of ugly painted faces, naked brown bodies, and a big stick that one of them wielded.

The newcomers laughed when they saw Thad. All were painted in what he came to know as the colors for war and death. Both their faces and bodies were striped and splotched with white and yellow and red. Some were in fanciful patterns. There were large areas painted in solid black, too. All they wore were moccasins and breechclouts, except for some who wore bear-claw necklaces and one or two who had headdresses of buffalo horns.

These were young braves, he discovered. Each had a rolled bearskin or buffalo robe on his horse. Thad had the feeling that he was the first white person his two captors had taken, for they were obviously boasting to the others of their bravery. He learned afterward that they had stumbled onto him as they were picking up pecans after a raid on the Morton Ranch seven miles up the creek.

Later, as they got on higher ground, he could see the smoke of the still-burning buildings, and he noticed with a sick heart evidences of three members of the family who had been killed by the braves.

During that day they were joined by other Indians. The newcomers, most of them older than Thad's captors, would pull him about by the arm, looking him over and talking among themselves. Eventually one of the chiefs issued an order, and the two who had captured Thad began to pull his clothes off him. The Indians then threw the captive astride a horse across whose bony back were tied a jangling collection of kitchen pots, pans, and iron skillets. With every movement of the horse their edges dug into Thad's flesh. Because his hands were tied, he could not shift them. His legs and back were rubbed raw at the end of the day's ride. As they rode, Thad thought with shame how he had been captured because of his own carelessness.

They traveled in a direction slightly north of west, and after two hours were joined by a hard-riding band of twelve more braves, who were driving a loose herd of sixteen horses. A familiar nicker from among them brought Thad's head around, and there was his poor Little-bit—again in the hands of the Indians she so despised. It did not make him feel any easier to remember that his actions were the cause of her being captured.

A boy only a little older than Thad was riding Little-bit, and he grinned triumphantly as he rode past as close as he could come. His name, Thad was later to learn, was Scar Pony, the name being taken from his claim of Thad's pony and the scar she bore on her hip.

Father had been right when he guessed that it was a boy who had taken a fancy to Little-bit, and who stole her back as often as she escaped from him. Thad was boiling with anger inside, but he was not about to risk another beating, so he kept still. He was hurting from head to foot, but the worst hurt of all came from seeing Scar Pony astride Little-bit.

Comanches' Boy

6

ONE thing Thad had not liked at home was going over and over Scripture verses until he had them fixed in his memory. When he had complained about having to learn the texts, his father had said, "The Scriptures were given to man to guide and comfort him, but if you don't know them, they will never be of much help to you."

The meaning of the words he memorized had not always been clear to Thad. But an order is an order, so he had memorized them.

Now as he rode laced to the back of the Indian pony, his hands tied behind him, his body and legs raw and burning, his head sore and aching, he thought of what pa had said. But he was too dazed to be able to remember anything but his misery and his bitter hatred of his captors.

They rode until dark, then stopped in a little draw. No supper fire was made. The Comanches had jerky of buffalo meat, and a little pemmican. They gave Thad some of it plus a handful of parched corn and some pecans.

They had left behind them the country familiar to Thad, with its deep-banked creeks bordered with elm and pecan trees. They had passed through country of rolling prairie and low ridges such as he knew at home, where great old live-oak trees rose out of a deep sea of grass, and were now in scrub-oak country. It was not very pretty. Every hill had a heap of rocks sticking up on its top.

Here in this draw was a heap of rocks that seemed to tumble down the ravine. Halfway to the summit of the hill was a cluster of those boulders that formed a wall around three sides of an enclosure. Thad's Indian guard, a young fellow with the usual mask of war paint and meanness, pulled him from his horse's back. By this time Thad was a bleeding, bruised bundle of raw misery. The Indian pushed the stumbling boy ahead of him, over the rocks to the little enclosure. Thad motioned with his bound hands to him.

Spotted Boy and the Comanches

"I can't climb over these rocks with my hands tied," he shouted, hoping that the louder he yelled, the more likely he was to be understood. But the Indian only grinned maliciously and shoved him on.

An older Indian who seemed to be the leader of the little band had heard Thad. Evidently he understood something of the white man's language, for he gave a sharp command to the boy's captor, whose name, Thad learned later, was Two Lances. Then he stepped over and untied the rawhide thongs that bound Thad's hands. They were sore and numb, and Thad stretched his fingers, bending and unbending them until he could get a hold on the rocks.

The older man then brought Thad a breechclout, a worn pair of moccasins, and a piece of moth-eaten buffalo hide.

"Put on!" he ordered. Two Lances pushed the boy into the enclosure among the high rocks and motioned him to lie down. Thad drew his piece of buffalo hide about his shivering body and obeyed. It was the first of their commands that he was more than glad to obey.

Thad's captors had put in a long and busy day, and were soon fast asleep. Before Thad's guard lay down, he had tied the captive's ankles together with a thong of buckskin and attached this to his own wrist.

"Like hobbling a horse," Thad muttered to himself.

The breast of Two Lances, lying across the opening in the cluster of rocks, was soon rising and falling in a regular rhythm. But although Thad was dead tired, hungry, and sore, he could not go to sleep.

Thad had been looking for a way to escape ever since Two Lances and his friend had captured him, but now he lay weak and exhausted, discouraged and afraid. He called to mind stories of the Comanches' torture of white captives. He remembered One-Eye Johnny Ainsworth's disfigured face and what had happened to little Celie and her mother. He realized then how foolish he had been to venture so far away from Travis and Little-bit that morning.

He thought with trembling of what might be in store for him, and how his parents and brothers would be worrying about him. He was afraid they might risk their own lives trying to rescue him. Stark fear took hold of him until he recalled what his father had said about learning Scripture texts: "They can never do you any good if you don't know them." He began to pray in earnest that God would help him.

Suddenly something happened that he was never able to explain afterward. Later some people insisted that it was only a dream. But he knew what happened, for he was wide awake.

A voice sounded in his ears, a strong, clear voice that seemed to come from just behind him. It said, "I will never leave thee, nor forsake thee."

He lay still, his eyes wide open, tense, listening. The voice came again. "The angel of the Lord encampeth round about them that fear Him, and delivereth them." The words were texts of Scripture he had learned months ago. He waited, thinking, with more hope than he had yet felt. He had not understood those texts until now. He thought of how the Comanches had beaten him with a stick when he whimpered and had beaten him even harder when he cried out from pain. He was afraid that tomorrow he might cry out again, so he added this to his prayer, "And please, Lord, don't let me show these Indians that I'm afraid."

He thought this over, for it did not seem quite the right thing to ask. Then he thought of an improvement. "Dear Lord, don't let me *be* afraid."

He went to sleep then, with a feeling that help would come.

Awakening early, he remembered Melissa and his desire to find her and rescue her from the Comanches. He prayed, "Help me find Melissa, Lord, and get her away from the Comanches."

Thad had asked the Lord alone to deliver *him,* yet he wanted God to deliver Melissa with his—Thad's—help. But this did not occur to him then.

Two Lances stirred and sat up. A call came from outside. He loosed Thad's legs and yanked him to his feet, then pushed him

Spotted Boy and the Comanches

ahead of him into the camp. Morning had come, another hard day!

They crossed the Colorado that day, and after that Thad was in country entirely new to him. Every morning he was kicked awake at daylight and his ankles unbound. After a breakfast of jerky, pemmican, or parched corn, they traveled toward the west. After the fourth day the Comanches decided that they were not being followed, or that, if they were, their trackers had lost their trail. They shot an antelope, and once a day thereafter a fire was made and a hasty stew of antelope meat was prepared.

They had been traveling six days when a band of twenty or thirty braves joined them, coming in from farther southeast. They drove a herd of about two hundred horses. Since all wore brands, Thad knew they had been stolen. None of the brands, however, were familiar to him. Judging from the direction from which they had come and the fact that he was not acquainted with the brands, he figured they had been stolen in San Saba or McCulloch counties.

As Thad rode along he thought of his father's words: "If you don't know the Scriptures, they will never be a help to you."

At this time, with so few men to guard the frontier, the Comanches sometimes raided as far east and south as San Antonio.

From his brothers Thad had learned some of the Indian sign language as well as certain Comanche words. His brothers had been merely passing time when they taught the words to him. But now the knowledge served him well. It was easy for the boy to pick up strange words, so, with what he already knew, he learned the Comanche language rapidly. He spoke to his captors in their own tongue whenever possible, and it seemed to please them. Some of them took the trouble to teach him still more.

The newcomers told how they had taken several captives, among whom were a woman and two boys. They said they had to kill

them because they fought so hard. Thad was able to understand what they were saying.

As he lay at night on the ground, hungry, cold, and homesick, Thad tried to recall Scripture texts that might encourage him. One night the words of John 14:13 came to his mind: "Whatsoever ye shall ask in My name, that will I do." He tried to hold onto that as a promise for himself and to believe that help would come. The ninety-first psalm came to mind, especially the verse that says, "Thou shalt not be afraid for the terror by night; nor for the arrow that flieth by day."

He realized that he had not really felt fear since the first night, when he had asked to be kept from fear. That, he believed, was why Two Lances and the others had kept him alive and did not beat him anymore. They respected courage. He kept a cheerful face, obeying orders as though it was what he wanted to do.

Thad saw Little-bit every day, but it was no comfort to him. After the second day her bridle and saddle had been transferred to the horse ridden by Red Wolf, father of Scar Pony. Every little while during the day Scar Pony would rein Little-bit close beside the pony Thad was riding and give Thad a big grin. It irritated the captive boy at first, and he wondered if Scar Pony was trying to frighten him or merely gloating over the stolen pony. After a time he realized that the grin was more mischievously friendly than it was malicious. It was a sort of teasing grin. Thad had the feeling he had seen that face before, but he could not remember where.

Little-bit's mouth was bloody from the jaw rope the Indians used on her as they did on their other horses, and it made Thad furious. But there was nothing he could do about it.

His own troubles had eased some since he had quit showing fear. Two Lances no longer bound his ankles at night. Though Thad still rode surrounded by a load of rough tools and utensils, he learned to shift them around so that they were not so uncomfortable.

Thad often wondered if he would see Melissa, though he had no assurance that she was alive. He knew there were many bands of Comanches in west Texas and that, although they might get together at times, the chances were small that he would find himself with the same band that held her captive. He had also heard that many of the white captives of the Comanches were sold as slaves to the Mexicans in New Mexico, and to other tribes of Indians.

By midmorning of the tenth day of travel, Thad knew they were getting close to the Comanche camp. A loud yammering of dogs could be heard almost a mile away. His heart was thumping as they rode toward the village. Dozens of tepees made of poles and painted buffalo hides rose in the plain beside a small stream. They looked like a forest of fat trees. There was a county-fair atmosphere about the setting, with the noise of welcoming drums and shouting, chattering people.

Thad wondered what lay ahead of him here among these wild-appearing people. There was a medley of odors to greet their nostrils in the village, including meat drying on racks, hides curing, and campfire smoke. Most of the odors were warm and homey. Mingled with the other odors was that of an incense made of dried sweetgrass, which infused a pleasant fragrance. With the Indians, this fragrance was a favorite.

As they rode into the village, a swarm of women and children, all talking at once, gathered about them. The women looked Thad over contemptuously, and the children spat at him and threw stones and sticks.

He looked about him in wonder as he dismounted from his horse. He was amazed at the height of the tepees and at their neatness and beautiful decorations. Here and there among them was a tethered horse, and he noticed that all were in good condition. They were decorated with paint, ribbons, and feathers. These, he supposed, must be the favorite horses of some of the villagers, for he had seen a great herd of horses out on the plain beyond the village as they were approaching.

Thad was taken before the village chief, to whom Two Lances was apparently presenting him as a gift. The chief was a tall man for a Comanche, rather on the portly side, wearing a great bonnet of eagle feathers. His hair was in two braids that hung almost to his knees. The braids, woven with strips of bright-red flannel, were extended by strips of beaver fur and ornamented with silver disks. His buckskin garments were beautifully decorated with embroidery of beads and dyed porcupine quills.

The captive boy, however, was too worried about his own situation to see all this. He saw only the magnificence of the impressive figure and the frightening effect of the painted lines on his face. The chief was surrounded by braves of all ages, painted and ornamented, though with less splendor than Yellow Cloud.

Red Wolf, father of Scar Pony, who had been in charge of the raiding party that had taken Thad captive, had halted his band just before entering the village. These Indians, too, had donned feathers and war paint for their entry. Now he was talking to Yellow Cloud, and Thad was able to understand some of the conversation.

Red Wolf turned to him. Pointing to the chief, he said, "Yellow Cloud his name."

Yellow Cloud glared at the captive boy, then issued an order. Two Lances and another of the braves, each holding Thad by an arm, led the boy to the center of the village.

"Now," he thought, "I must not show them that I am afraid." He looked straight ahead, praying inwardly for protection.

The yammering crowd of villagers followed, shouting insults, spitting, and lashing with sticks and whips of braided leather. He was in a daze from blows on his head by the time he was tied to a stake and wood was piled about his feet for a fire.

There for a time he was used as a target for stones, sticks, and whips. Several women jabbed him with short-handled spears. There seemed to be no intention of hitting him in a vital spot. They were having their fun with him before they finished him off, he guessed.

Thad was near to losing consciousness, although he had not once cried out from pain. Before the torchbearers had reached him, a stir in the crowd caused him to look about. A woman, plump and motherly appearing, was screaming shrilly at the crowd and pushing her way toward him. She seemed to be addressing some of her remarks to Yellow Cloud.

The chief issued an order then, and, as suddenly as it had begun, the captive's abuse ceased. He was profoundly grateful to the woman, whoever she was.

Two Lances, grinning broadly, untied the thongs that bound Thad to the post and led him to Yellow Cloud.

With Blue Flower, he spent days on his hands and knees scraping
the hides with a hoe-shaped implement. It was a job he detested.

Life With Little Rabbit 7

Y ELLOW CLOUD led the boy to his tepee. The woman who had called for his release trotted along behind. Thad was so weak that he could barely stumble along. The woman, he saw, was the wife of Yellow Cloud. Her name, he learned, was Little Rabbit.

When they reached the lodge of the chief, he turned to Thad and said, "You obey this woman."

To Little Rabbit he said, "This boy—he is yours. You make him work."

Though he did not understand all the words of the chief, Thad knew well enough what was meant. He had heard of the custom of giving a captive to a woman. Thad was Little Rabbit's slave. To a boy of the Comanches, it was the supreme insult to be ordered about by a woman. To Thad it meant nothing of the kind. He had carried out his mother's orders all his life. She had called him her "righthand man," and he had been proud of the title. Besides, he knew that he owed his life to Little Rabbit, and for that he would serve her gratefully.

Another woman sat in front of the adjoining lodge, working at her embroidery on a buckskin pouch while her baby swung peacefully in a hand-embroidered cradle. The cradle was a bag into which the little fellow was laced in a standing position. It hung by two decorated buckskin straps from a nearby oak tree. Little Rabbit was dressed in a fringed and beaded garment of doeskin, but the other, whose name was Blue Flower, wore a white woman's dress of calico.

Little Rabbit gave Blue Flower an order in a crisp, commanding tone, and she obeyed at once.

"Is Blue Flower your daughter?" Thad asked Little Rabbit, who must have been near his mother's age.

"Yellow Cloud's other woman," was Little Rabbit's reply. So

the chief had two wives! Thad had heard of that Indian custom before.

When he entered Little Rabbit's lodge, Thad was amazed at the neatness of its arrangement and the beauty of the furnishings. He had always thought that an Indian lodge would be a mere dirty shelter, but here were neatness and order. The lodge had a buckskin lining upon which had been painted the stories of various battles and hunting experiences. The colors were bright. About the inside were brightly painted objects of daily use, such as war drums, saddlebags, carrying cases, willow backrests, and robes and pillows for a couch. A fire burned in the middle of the hard-packed floor.

Little Rabbit gently washed the boy's wounds, and that night, on an old buffalo robe thrown on the floor, he slept the sleep of total exhaustion.

The next morning, with no consideration for Thad's weakened condition, Little Rabbit put him to work.

"Get wood!" was her first command. Thad had begun his period of servitude in the camp of the Comanches.

Thad made up his mind that Little Rabbit should have no reason to complain of his work, and after a few weeks, life became easier. At first Little Rabbitt seemed to be trying him out, keeping him at work all day bringing water, fetching wood, and scraping hides. At least, after a few weeks he was no longer kicked to his feet each morning by Yellow Cloud.

Little Rabbit brought him a surprise gift one day. It was a suit of clothes. Besides the breechclout there was a pair of buckskin leggings and a tunic that came down over them almost to his knees. Now he would not only be warm, but his fair skin would be protected from the sun's burning rays.

"These," said Little Rabbit, "are the garments of my son."

"Have you a son?" Thad asked, surprised. He had seen no one in the village who seemed to be a son of Little Rabbit and Yellow Cloud.

"My son is dead," Little Rabbit said. "Long Knives killed him."

"How did it happen?" he asked.

"In a battle last year. Our men had gone to take horses and white men found them. My son died."

Thad remembered. It must have been at the Austin ranch. The Indians had been raiding and burning, and a young buck was killed there. But he said nothing, for Little Rabbit believed that whatever the men of her tribe had done was the right thing. To her, the Long Knives were always in the wrong.

As he worked, Thad looked about him at the women and girls, hoping to find one with clear blue eyes and a soft, dark cloud of curly hair. But the girls he saw wore their straight black hair cut short at the neck. This was the custom of Comanche women.

Every day, when Thad went to find wood, Blue Flower accompanied him, while Little Rabbit watched the baby. He had hoped that while getting wood or water he could circulate about a little and maybe find Melissa. After a few weeks Blue Flower relaxed her watchfulness, and he was able to get away a little more each day.

Yellow Cloud and Little Rabbit talked to him these days, too. He was becoming one of them.

"You are no longer a boy of the Long Knives," Yellow Cloud said one day. "You will soon be a boy of the Comanches."

Thad said nothing, for he was afraid to say what he was thinking.

"You will see," said Yellow Cloud, "that the white man makes war against the Comanches. We must fight back because this is our land. For many years we have hunted here."

Thad knew the purpose behind such talk. Johnny Ainsworth had warned him that the Indians tried to turn captives against their own people. Thad made up his mind that he would pretend to believe them. But he was determined that he would never be influenced by their words. He kept remembering little Celie, her mother, and Johnny Ainsworth's face. He was still sure he hated the Comanches.

There came a day when he thought he had found Melissa. He saw a little Comanche girl wearing a white girl's dress which he recognized. It was blue-and-white-striped with little pink roses scattered over it. Either Melissa was somewhere in this camp or she was no longer alive. He searched the face of every girl he saw, but not one looked like Melissa Branson.

Coming home from gathering wood one day, he passed a crowd of boys playing a game. It consisted of trying to ring a pole stuck upright in the ground, with a hoop made from a willow twig. He stopped to watch them.

Scar Pony saw him and called out so that all could hear, "Long Knife boy is woman!"

Thad had an answer for that. "Scar Pony is woman, ride woman horse." He knew that no grown Comanche man would ride a mare. Mares were for women.

"I will never ride woman horse after I am a man," Scar Pony argued.

"Why do you steal her from me, then, whenever she runs away from you?" Thad demanded.

"I do not steal what is already mine," Scar Pony retorted. "I want her so I may have other ponies like her someday. Then I will ride only her sons."

Thad asked why the Indian boy had shot her full of arrows; but Scar Pony denied having done that.

Scar Pony changed the subject. "You white boy got spots on face."

Thad ran his hand over his freckle-spattered cheeks and nose. "Freckles," he said.

"Running Fox and I call you 'Spotted Boy,'" Scar Pony said. "We think that is good name."

Thad grinned good-naturedly. "As good as any, I reckon." He rather liked the name. Until now Yellow Cloud and Little Rabbit had dubbed him "Snow on Top," because of his white hair. He liked "Spotted Boy" better.

"You steal my pony, Blackbird," Scar Pony said after a little.

"I didn't have to steal her," Thad said. "She knows where she belongs, and she came home to me by herself."

"Maybe my father, Red Wolf, sell her to Comancheros in New Mexico," Scar Pony said next.

"Why hasn't he sold her before this?" Thad asked. It was something he had wondered about, for he knew that many of the stolen horses were driven into Mexico or New Mexico. The animals were sold to the Mexicans along the Rio Grande who were known as "Comancheros" because they traded with Comanches.

"I did not want him to sell Blackbird," Scar Pony said. "My father will not sell her if I do not want him to."

So that was it! Thad had to yield a sort of wry gratitude to the Indian boy. Had not Scar Pony wanted Little-bit for raising future ponies, she would have been sold long ago to the Comancheros and Thad would never have seen her again.

Several times after that Scar Pony came to Yellow Cloud's lodge and asked permission for Thad to come and take part in the boys' games. Sometimes Little Rabbit shook her head and set Thad at a new task, but other times she permitted him to go.

All one afternoon they practiced shooting arrows at a mark on a cottonwood tree. At first Thad's arrows went so wide that the others laughed. It was hard to get the hang of it, although with rifle or pistol he was as quick and accurate as any man at home.

After a while he began to sense the direction and strength of the wind, and gradually he improved until he was almost as skilled as the Comanche boys.

"Someday," Scar Pony confided, "you will go with us on the hunt." Thad grasped at this promise with joy, for he had watched the Indian boys galloping over the hills and plains on their ponies, or returning from the hunt with their older brothers. He had envied them their freedom, and wondered if Little Rabbit would ever let him go with them.

Now that Running Fox, Scar Pony, and some of the other boys were friendly to him, Thad's life was not so hard. Almost daily Little Rabbit gave him time to play for an hour or two. The boys got into discussions of all sorts, and Thad took the opportunity one day to ask about something he had wondered about. "Why," he asked, "do you Comanches raid and steal and kill the white people when the government has given you a place in Indian Territory north of the Red River? Don't they feed you and give you land to work?"

Scar Pony's older brother Whirlwind spat on the ground and replied with a sneer, "Do the Long Knives own the world? The Comanches for many generations have called this land their own. We have hunted where we would. Now the Long Knives would keep us on small lands far from our hunting grounds. We do not like that. We go where we want to. We like to hunt where we have always hunted."

Thad had to admit to himself, much as he hated to, that he would not like such an arrangement either.

Some time later a band of Indians approached. They were greeted with a clamor of welcome, so Thad judged them to belong to Yellow Cloud's village. They were leading ponies loaded with buffalo meat and hides. Thad recognized them then. They were young men just returning from the hunt.

Now he was made to do more squaws' work, scraping hides and preparing them for curing. The fresh hides were stretched on the ground or a standing frame and pegged taut with stout wooden pegs. With Blue Flower, he spent days on his hands and knees scraping the hides with a hoe-shaped implement of horn or buffalo shoulder bone. All the bits of flesh and fat that clung to the hides were removed. It was a job Thad detested, and it left him sore and exhausted by nightfall. He also spent many hours cutting the meat into strips for drying.

Although Thad had already accumulated a large heap of wood for the winter, he was still sent out for more. The need would be great when the weather grew colder. Little Rabbit had stacked the wood neatly just inside the door of the lodge.

Hunting for more wood one evening, he had to go some distance from camp. There was little timber in the country, and the Comanches burned mostly the low-growing mesquite and buffalo chips.

As Thad was stooping to pick up a piece of dead wood, a voice spoke to him from the brush nearby. "Thad Conway," the voice said, "don't let them see us talking."

He looked about as a girl stepped from the bushes. At first glance the girl looked like all the others: straight, short black hair and dark skin, though not quite as dark as that of the others. She was dressed only in an uneven tunic of buckskin. A pair of old moccasins were tied to her feet. He had seen this sorry-looking figure about the camp, but had thought nothing of it. He had taken her for a Comanche child. He should have recognized that she was not dressed as warmly or as neatly as the other children.

Looking again, he noted that her eyes were deep blue in color. These were no Indian eyes! It was, it had to be, Melissa Branson! His heart skipped several beats and his voice sounded strange as he managed to say, "Lissy, I didn't know you! What happened to your hair?"

"They cut it and rubbed bear grease in it to make it straight so I'd look like all the others." She seemed to be groping for the words as though speaking in a language new to her. Thad hardly knew what to say, the meeting was so sudden.

"Don't let them see us talking together," she repeated. "They'll kill us. Buffalo Horn has warned me never to speak to you."

Thad turned to break the stick he was about to add to his load. His thoughts were not working, but somewhere inside he felt a lightness, as if the ground would not stay under his feet. He had found Melissa!

"How did they get you?" she asked, stooping to pick up some buffalo chips to put into her basket. "Did they burn your house and kill your folks?"

"No, I was on the creek with Travis, after cattle. I was picking up pecans and we got separated. I think Trav got away." Then a thought occurred to Thad. Did Melissa know Celie was dead?

"How did they happen to keep you alive?" he asked her.

"I reckon because my hair is dark," she answered. "And I didn't cry. I was too scared to cry." They worked at their wood gathering for a few moments without speaking. Thad believed that both of them had Celie in mind.

Suddenly Melissa burst out crying. Thad tried to comfort her in his awkward way, putting his arm around her while she cried on his shoulder. He felt a love for little Lissy Branson such as he had never known before. He longed to help her, but they were a forlorn pair of children with no help in sight.

After a little he said what had been on his mind ever since he had been taken by Two Lances and his friend on the creek.

"Melissa, we've got to run away," Thad said finally.

"But how?" she asked.

"I don't know for sure," Thad replied. "But now that I've found you, I'll think of a way."

A sound in the bushes told them Blue Flower and the other women and girls were coming. Melissa turned and hurried toward them.

"We won't ever speak to each other in camp," Thad whispered as she was leaving. She made no answer except to shake her head. Thad hastily got his load of wood on his back and hurried in the opposite direction. After that, whenever he saw the forlorn little figure about the village, he gave no sign that he knew her. But he watched morning and evening to see which way she went for wood and water. When she seemed to be alone, he tried to get close to her without attracting attention. He found only a few opportunities to speak to her in safety. All he could say then were the whispered words, "I'm still trying to figure out a way for us to get home again."

At night Thad would try to think up plans for their escape. Generally he was too tired, and would fall into a deep sleep as soon as he had rolled himself in his buffalo robe. But during the day he was constantly thinking of escape.

He realized that the first thing they must have was a horse apiece. Little-bit he *must* have. He was almost as anxious to free the horse as he was to save Melissa. No doubt Little-bit, smooth customer that she was, would have escaped long ago if Thad had not been close by, thought the boy.

One day as he was on his way back to camp, stooping under a heavy load of wood, he was grumbling to himself about the way he was being treated. And this despite the fact that Yellow Cloud and Little Rabbit were treating him better every day. "Hauling wood like a mule!" he thought.

Suddenly he had an inspiration. Throwing the wood down beside the lodge, he said to Little Rabbit, "I go far for this wood, farther each day. It is growing scarce near camp. Comanche women have horse to bring wood. I need horse. Bring more wood with horse."

Little Rabbit's eyes crinkled maliciously. "No horse," she said. Then, striking Thad across the shoulders with a piece of stiff hide, she added, "Spotted Boy good horse."

Thad tried to grin at her joke, but it didn't sound even slightly funny. His request paid off, however, for the next day when he started out for wood, Little Rabbit said, "Spotted Boy, get horse."

He grabbed a rawhide hackamore and hurried to where the horse herd grazed some distance from camp. Most of the horses were hobbled and could not stray far, but they were also under a guard of half-grown boys and one or two men.

Little-bit came jumping toward him as fast as she could travel. She was impeded by her hobbles, but when she saw him coming, she gave a loving nicker and rubbed her head against his shoulder. He petted her, smoothing her silken nose and rubbing her neck. She was a link with home. He loved her almost as much as he did the members of his family. He ran his hand over her muzzle and touched her sore jaw tenderly.

"You'll help me haul wood, won't you, Little-bit?" Thad was slipping the hackamore on her when Scar Pony came running toward him.

"Blackbird my horse!" he shouted. "You will not take my horse!"

Never had Thad wanted so much to clout anyone over the head, and he swung the braided hackamore in his hand. He knew he must go along in a good humor with anything the Comanches required of him, but he could not resist starting an argument with the Indian.

Spotted Boy and the Comanches

"This horse is not 'Blackbird.' Her name is 'Little-bit.' In Comanche that means 'Small Thing.' You steal her from me."

"Always she is my pony," Scar Pony said in a quarrelsome tone. "My people lose her when she was too tired. You Long Knives find her. She is not yours."

"She is mine. She would have died. I keep her alive. Now you steal her from me."

Scar Pony laughed. "Many times I steal," he boasted. "Now I keep."

Thad realized that this talk might defeat his purpose, so he changed his tack. "No good, this horse," he said. "You keep."

He looked about at the other horses, thinking this would be a good opportunity to select one that would later help him escape. He had decided that Lissy should ride Little-bit, for she was gentle and had an easy gait. More important, she would head straight for home, so that if they should become separated Melissa would not get lost.

Now Thad selected a dark-brown horse with a sturdy body and legs long enough to outdistance any of the others. As he rode him, Thad talked gently, stroked his mane, and patted his neck. Loading the wood on the animal's back, Thad was careful to fasten it so that it would not chafe the hide.

Thad called the horse "Bullet," and tried to make him feel that he belonged to him. He had inquired of the boys of the horse guard if this one belonged to any warrior in particular. It would only make the Indians' pursuit of Melissa and him more determined if he were riding anyone's favorite horse. When it came to Little-bit, he would simply have to take the chance.

Perhaps it was because Little Rabbit had begun to think of Thad as a son; or maybe it was because Bullet helped get the wood faster. Whatever the reason, she began to lighten up on his other tasks, and he had more time to play.

On an afternoon as Thad was busy scraping a hide, Little Rabbit sat with some of the other women sewing the seams on a buffalo-hide lodge cover. One of the women said to Little Rabbit,

"Your new son has hair like the snow." The other women laughed and joked her about the spots on her boy's face, as well as his cottonlike hair.

When they had gone to their lodges, Little Rabbit set about changing things. She dyed Thad's hair with some sort of walnut-juice extract and rubbed enough of it on his face to hide his freckles. Then she braided his hair into two braids, extending them with weavings of cloth and adorning them with red and green feathers. When he looked into the pool that evening, he saw the strange reflection of an Indian boy with light-blue eyes. Who would recognize him as Thad Conway now? He was not sure whether he was pleased or displeased.

Now Scar Pony and Running Fox began treating him more as one of them. He came to be as skillful as any with bow and arrow, and often brought home a rabbit or a few quail for Little Rabbit's pot. She seemed proud of his accomplishments. Even Yellow Cloud commended him on his marksmanship.

Although Scar Pony was more friendly toward the white boy, it made Thad boil inside to see Little-bit under the Indian boy's rein. He did manage to show the Indian lad that it was cruel to use a jaw rein on her. When Thad first talked to him about it, he replied with a contemptuous twist of his mouth, "Pony him no hurt."

"It does, too, hurt a pony, the same as it would hurt you!" Thad argued. But Scar Pony jumped on her back and rode away as though unimpressed. However, from that time on Thad noticed that she wore a bit and bridle.

Scar Pony was something of a dandy in a Comanche sort of way. He kept his hair neatly braided, with bright feathers stuck in it. When he rode Little-bit, he stuck dyed hawk or eagle feathers in her mane. Thad had to admit that the two presented a jaunty appearance.

The Comanche boys had many games, and Thad now found time to take part in them. One was the game with a willow hoop. In another they used corncobs with three turkey feathers stuck in the small end. These they attempted to cast through a hoop at some distance or used as a dart to aim at targets. Pine cones were used for toss and catch. Certain games were designed to develop warrior skills. One of these featured a shield and rawhide-covered ball. One player held an old shield on his arm, as he stood in the center of a large circle marked on the ground. With his shield he tried to avoid being hit by the balls being thrown at him from outside the circle. The player who first struck his body with a ball took his place.

The Comanche boys' heroes were the men most skillful in the hunt or the raid, who brought home the most buffalo or antelope. The boys worked hard at games that increased these skills.

Thad was happily surprised one day when Scar Pony came running to greet him. "We go on a hunt for antelope tomorrow," Scar Pony told him. "Little Rabbit says you go with us."

Thad had not built his hopes on Scar Pony's promise, made him some time ago, to take him along on a hunt. Now he was full of excitement.

Yellow Cloud took down from its loop on the wall a bow encased in a finely worked hide case. From behind his backrest he brought a quiver full of arrows.

"You take these, my son," he said. "These were used by our other son."

Before dark settled down, Thad practiced firing at a target with his new bow and arrows. He hoped to be as successful as the other boys on the hunt. Perhaps then they would consider taking him on a buffalo hunt someday. To hunt a buffalo was something he had always wanted to do.

The Hunters

THAD rode Bullet, not from choice but because Scar Pony was riding Little-bit. Thad made no argument about it; he was biding his time. He had adorned Bullet with feathers and paint. Except for certain thoughts inside, he felt like a real Comanche. He could not have looked much like an Indian boy, for the walnut dye was wearing off his freckles and his light-colored hair was growing in again. Several of the young braves went with them, their bodies bare except for breechclout and moccasins and a few feathers in their hair. A buffalo robe was rolled and tied to the back of each saddle. The nights were still cold, although spring was on the way.

Reaching the region where scouts had reported antelope, they searched the horizon. At last one of the young men called with suppressed excitement, "They go there!"

Whistling Dog and one of the other braves each put an antelope's head, complete with horns, on his head. It gave a realistic imitation of a living antelope.

The hunters dropped from their ponies and left them with one of the boys. Then they crept toward the slope where the game had been spotted, each holding a dried tumbleweed in front of him.

Soon Whistling Dog gave them a signal to lie quietly where they were. They watched until a head appeared not far away. Then a white rump showed as the animal turned his back toward the hunters.

Whistling Dog slowly raised his lance with a white cloth attached to its point. This he held very still. The only movement was the fluttering of the cloth in the breeze. Antelope are curious creatures and will risk their lives to investigate something strange.

The antelope on the slope threw up his head again, and almost immediately eight or ten more heads appeared. Then they were lowered again as the animals resumed their grazing. Again

Spotted Boy and the Comanches

Whistling Dog raised the lance. The first antelope took a step or two toward the hunters while the others watched. Whenever the antelope lowered their heads to graze again, the hunters crept silently forward. Finally they were within easy arrow shot. Whistling Dog raised his mask, and every one of the hunters let fly with an arrow at an animal already selected.

It was hard to tell who had scored hits, but seven antelope went down. Most of them were shot through the neck. The other antelope, including the one at which Thad had aimed, were off in a flash, their white rumps bobbing across the plain.

The hunters jumped to their feet. They ran for a moment in the direction the antelope had taken. Then they turned back to the skinning of those they had shot. Now the hour was late, and the hunters were far from home. They decided to make camp for the night where they were.

Cutting ribs from one of the antelope, they roasted them over a fire of buffalo chips. While the meat cooked, the hunters stretched their tired bodies in the warm glow of the fire. They talked as men and boys of any race love to talk on such an occasion.

Scar Pony and Thad sat beside each other, each holding a piece of meat on a forked stick. It was a time when friendly talk, even between enemies, came easy. Scar Pony kept up a running conversation with Thad, most of it about the events of the day. Then he said, "Spotted Boy, I saw you before Two Lances found you at the creek."

"When did you ever see me?" Thad asked.

"With Long Arrow I followed you and the two women on the horses. We shot arrows at you, but we did not try to hit you. Our men were a long way off. It was only to see you run."

"I don't remember riding far with two women," Thad said.

"One woman was young. She had two little ones. The older woman took one of the little ones on her saddle when you heard the drums from our camp," Scar Pony explained. "You were riding my Blackbird."

Then Thad remembered. It was the day that they had been

to visit the Bransons, ma and Mis' Ellie Clark and the little ones.

"The older woman was my mother," Thad said. "But when did you see me besides that time?"

"Once when you and your dogs and some boys of the Long Knives had a raccoon treed. The dogs fought the raccoon, and he almost drowned one of them."

"Oh!" said Thad. "One was my brother and the other was the brother of the white girl who lives in Buffalo Horn's lodge. They call her 'Sleep-Walk Girl.' You were laughing at us."

"We laughed at the dogs and the raccoon," Scar Pony explained.

"I remember well," Thad said. "I felt as though someone were looking at me, and when I looked up, I saw you. But I didn't know until now that it was you." He remembered that he had noticed the friendly expression on the face of one of the three Comanche boys that day, even as Scar Pony's face now wore a look of friendship.

"Who were the others with you?" Thad asked.

"Running Fox and Boy Who Laughs were there," Scar Pony answered. "But there were others, older men, in the woods behind us. We did not want a fight then. The warriors were planning an attack on a ranch before morning."

Thad laughed. "It's a good thing for us that you didn't want a fight. We boys were alone and had little ammunition."

"I, too, am glad we did not fight," Scar Pony agreed, "or you would not be my friend now."

One of the things about the Comanches that Thad disliked was their boastfulness. After a buffalo hunt or a raid, the men told long-winded stories around the village fires, pompously describing their brave deeds. Two Lances and his friend had even made a great story of their courage in capturing Thad at the creek. It was ridiculous to think it took any great bravery to capture a lone boy by surprise.

Whistling Dog and another young warrior, Rising Bear, were listening now to the conversation of the two boys. Whistling Dog spoke to Thad.

Spotted Boy and the Comanches

"I have seen in the houses of the Long Knives the books that talk. Do books talk to you?"

For a moment Thad did not understand what Whistling Dog meant. Then it dawned on him. He was asking if Thad could read.

He nodded his head. "Yes, they talk to me," he said.

"I have heard that the Long Knives have a great Book from the heavens," said Whirlwind. He had waited a long time before speaking of this, and the pause showed the importance he attached to his words. Following this custom, Thad took his time to answer Whirlwind. He hoped thus to convince him that he considered this part of the conversation important, too.

The hunters listened to him as he answered. "We have such a Book," he said.

"What does the talking Book from the heavens tell you?" Whistling Dog asked.

Another long wait during which the boy appeared to be thinking. Then Thad answered, "The Book tells us many things about the God who lives beyond the sun. He made the sun."

"The sun gives us life," Whistling Dog said.

"The sun merely warms us," Thad replied.

"Does the Book tell how we may defeat our enemies?" Whirlwind asked.

Thad gave this some long thought. He was trying to recall some of the Scripture texts he had learned, but not one would come to mind. The eyes of the other hunters were upon him, waiting for his answer. Finally he had an inspiration. "The Book tells us that the Father God sent His Son from heaven to tell us that we must love everybody. We must love even our enemies." As he spoke the words, Thad thought of the hatred he had felt for these, his enemies. He was not paying heed to the teachings of the Book himself.

A long silence followed during which the boys and young men sat with bowed heads. He wondered what they were thinking. At last Whistling Dog spoke, quite reasonably. "If we love our enemy, he is no longer our enemy. How, then, can we kill him?"

Thad pondered this question, then answered, "I reckon we couldn't."

The subject was something beyond his power to explain and perhaps, he thought, the others found it as difficult.

After a few bouts of wrestling, in which Thad could hold his own with any of the other boys his age, the hunters rolled themselves in their robes and slept beside the dying fire. Thad, looking up at the far stars that he had so often watched from home, felt himself a part of this wild life and these people. Still, there were times when he lay awake and longed for his own home and his own kind of people.

There were guns in Yellow Cloud's camp, but not enough for all the braves. To Thad it seemed that the Indians were better marksmen with bow and arrow or lance than with guns. He himself had never become as expert with bow and arrow as he was with a gun. So when Scar Pony told him there was to be a buffalo hunt and that the boys would be allowed to go along, he decided to ask Yellow Cloud for the use of one of the two guns that hung in his tepee.

"I am not so good at shooting with the bow and arrow as with the rifle," he explained.

Yellow Cloud asked, "Can you bring down the buffalo with the gun?"

"I think so," Thad answered, not wishing to make a definite promise.

"Many buffalo have been found," Yellow Cloud said. "They will soon be gone to the north, so we must get plenty meat for our women to dry."

"Then will you let me use the gun?" Thad asked again.

"Maybe gun, maybe bow," was all the answer he got from Yellow Cloud as he turned back into his lodge.

Before first daylight the following morning, Thad brought Bullet to the door of the lodge to saddle him for the hunt. As he did so, Yellow Cloud brought him the gun from behind his backrest. It was a muzzle-loader, of course, as were most rifles of the time. As

Spotted Boy and the Comanches

Thad sighted along the barrel, he wished he had been given time with it to get the feel of this one.

The hunters rode northward, following the buffalo herd. They came on the buffalo at midmorning, a vast black mass of animals grazing quietly in the sunshine. The hunters who had brought buffalo headgear now donned them and crept on foot toward their prey. The foolish buffalo scarcely lifted their heads, so it was easy for the hunters to approach them in their disguise. Thad guessed there were many thousands of the animals, for the black, slowly

moving mass reached as far as the eye could see and well beyond.

Thad was not at first permitted to fire his gun, for the Comanches had a system of buffalo hunting that to him seemed cruel. It kept the buffalo from becoming alarmed too soon, however, and enabled the hunters to get all the meat they needed before the animals should stampede. Running alongside the herd on their ponies, keeping pace with the buffalo, each lancer chose a beast and paced it until he had a good target. Suddenly he leaned forward, his lance raised in both hands, and drove it into the loins of the buffalo. A backward heave of the hunter's body brought the lance point free of the wounded animal, and it fell.

The poor beast was only wounded, and the lancer rode on after another target. He was followed by the boys and one or two old men who finished killing the wounded beasts with bow and arrow. Then some of the old men and the women came to skin the carcasses.

When at last the buffalo herd awoke to the fact that they were under attack, and were alarmed by the smell of blood, Red Wolf gave the signal to those who carried guns. Until now the slaughter had been silent. Now Thad, with the others who had guns, raced alongside the frightened, madly running horde of animals. Thad

shot one, dropped to the ground and reloaded, threw himself on his horse to race and shoot again. Several times he reloaded, raced, and shot, taking care that he hit a vital spot in each, aiming for the neck or a point just behind the shoulder. He left no wounded animals to await the mercy of death.

When the buffalo had departed and the killing halted, a mile or more had been covered by the hunters. Their trail was marked by the carcasses of fallen animals, with women and old men at work upon them.

The hunters washed themselves at a little stream and returned to the campfires. The women were already roasting fat humps and ribs of buffalo.

After a rest the boys, still excited from the hunt, started a hand-wrestling match. A boy placed the side of his foot against that of his opponent. Then, grasping hands, each endeavored to throw the other.

Thad had noticed how changeable and childish an Indian's moods might be. One moment Yellow Cloud might be laughing and joking with the women or playing with Blue Flower's baby. The next moment he might take offense at some small thing and give the offender a beating. At first Thad had been outraged at such treatment of a woman by a man, but it seemed to be the accustomed thing among the Indians. When it happened that Little Rabbit was the one punished, she would take out her ire on Blue Flower, slapping her, scolding her, and setting her at some difficult task. Sometimes it was Thad who caught the brunt of her anger.

Thad had wrestled often with the other boys. One of the best wrestlers was Small Weasel, about the same age and size as Thad. They were evenly matched and sometimes Thad had been thrown again and again by Small Weasel. Sometimes he had been able to throw the other boy. Today Thad threw Small Weasel three times in succession. Small Weasel was never the most handsome boy in Yellow Cloud's band; his eyes were small, glittering beads, close-set in a face that was heavily pockmarked. Now as he leaped to his feet after his third fall, his face was the mask of evil. Crazed with anger, and forgetting all the rules of the sport, he came up with a lance in his hand and threw it at Thad with all his might. Had it landed where he aimed, there would have been no more Spotted Boy; but Thad dodged just in time. It made only a deep flesh wound in the muscle of his upper arm. Small Weasel seized another lance, but Thad threw a rock at him, hitting Small Weasel in the forehead. The Indian boy dropped to the ground like a dead buffalo.

Thad, fearing that he had harmed the other boy more than he had intended, knelt over him. Chafing Small Weasel's hands, he called to Scar Pony, "Get water!"

Scar Pony came running with a gourd full of water. As Thad bathed the boy's face and head with it, Small Weasel opened his eyes and sat up, rubbing his head. He looked at Thad in surprise when he realized that the white boy was leaning over him, not to harm, but to help. Now Thad helped him to his feet and led him to the women at the campfire.

Scar Pony, Boy Who Laughs, and Running Fox were speechless with amazement at such behavior. In a perplexed tone of voice Scar Pony asked, "Why does Spotted Boy help his enemy? Small Weasel tried to kill you."

"Is it because you do as the Book from heaven tells you?" Boy Who Laughs wondered.

Thad shrugged his shoulders. He could not explain his action except to say he was brought up that way.

"Small Weasel is not my enemy," he said. "He was angry because I beat him at wrestling. Wouldn't you have helped him?"

The Indian boys shook their heads. Surely, they thought, the ways of the Long Knives were strange indeed.

Mis' Sally and the Twins 9

MELISSA hissed at Thad one morning as he passed near the lodge of Buffalo Horn. He slowed his steps. She walked past him and said in a low voice, "You know Mis' Sally Buchanan?"

"Sure, I know her. What about her?"

"I guess you heard that they took her and her two little grandsons captive when they raided the Buchanan ranch. She's in camp not far from here."

"We thought the Comanches had killed them all," Thad whispered, walking along slowly behind her. "How do you know she's alive?"

"I saw her. I went with Buffalo Horn and Talking Woman to the village of War Hawk. Chief War Hawk just made camp over on the other branch of this creek last night. Mis' Sally wants to talk to you. She will meet us at that water hole by the bend in the creek where all the willows grow."

That evening when he went for water, Thad slipped away from Blue Flower while she gossiped with the other women, and hurried to the creek. There was a good deal of underbrush there. It was about halfway between the villages of War Hawk and Yellow Cloud. He dallied at the water hole, hoping the Comanche girls and women would soon go away, as he knew that Mis' Sally would pretend not to see him if others were around.

Finally they all drifted away with their jars and buckets of water. Thad looked around and saw Mis' Sally coming from a clump of bushes. He scarcely recognized her, dressed as she was in a ragged doeskin dress. The sight of her warmed his heart as nothing else had done since he had first seen Melissa, for she was a vision of home.

"Law me, Thad!" she exclaimed, grinning gleefully. "This is a fine fix you've got yourself in."

Thad grinned back at her. "Looks like you're in sort of a fix yourself, Mis' Sally," he said. "How come they got you?"

Spotted Boy and the Comanches

"I'll tell you all about it, Thad. First I must see if those young ones, Tommy and Timmy, are a-coming."

She slipped back through the bushes and returned in a moment with her small grandsons. Thad would never have known them. They had black hair and dark-brown eyes to begin with. Now they wore little suits of buckskin, embroidered with bright-colored beads and dyed porcupine quills, with beautifully beaded moccasins. Their hair was long, and their skin was almost as dark as a Comanche child's from living in the sunshine. They could easily have passed for the well-loved sons of a Comanche chief.

"I made those little suits for them myself," Mis' Sally said. "And War Hawk's old woman did the trimming on them. You'd think they were her own young ones the way she pets and pampers them."

"They're mighty cute little shavers," Thad remarked. "I don't blame her for making over them."

"Well, I don't like it a little bit," Mis' Sally said. "They're looking more like little Injuns every day. I'm powerful anxious to get them away from these savages. Old War Hawk and White Clover, his woman, would like nothing better than to raise them to be their own sons and good Comanche braves. That's what will happen, too, if I don't get them away from here."

Thad told her of his plan to escape with Melissa. "Maybe you and the twins could escape with us," Thad suggested.

She shook her head. Mis' Sally was a practical woman.

"No, Thad, we would only hinder you. But I'll do whatever I can to help you two get away. I will hope, if you make it, that you'll tell my sons, Buck and Bill, where you saw us last and whose band we are with, so they can come and fetch us home. I'd walk off and take my chances of escaping from the red devils if I didn't have these little ones to think of."

"It's a wonder they left you alive when they raided your place," Thad said.

She laughed. "That's a story, boy. I just naturally captured myself, you might say. When I saw they were setting fire to the house, I ran out the back door with these two young ones in my arms.

88

A big Comanche buck knocked me down and snatched them away from me. When I got up and managed to get my breath again, I saw him running off with them, one under each arm, a-kickin' and a-squallin' like two bobcat kittens.

"I took off after him, madder than a wet hen, yelling at him in Comanche. I reckon he didn't know what to make of an old white woman yelling at him in his own language, so he turned to look at me."

"Did you throw a rock at him?" Thad asked, thinking that that was what he would have done.

"No," she said. "I didn't want to make him mad. I hollered at him, 'Let me go with you and I'll take care of those papooses for you!' He turned and ran again and I followed him to where he got back on his horse. I was afraid one of the bunch would knock my brains out, so I hid until they all got together and started off."

Thad was tingling with the excitement of her story.

"Well, sir," Mis' Sally went on, "I followed the band until they made their first night's camp. They went faster than I could, so it was late when I finally got to their camping place by following their tracks. I hid for the rest of the night in the bushes close by, and in the morning I went into their camp and told them I was going along with them. I reckon they thought I was a mite out of my head, or else that I just naturally hankered for life in a Comanche village. They didn't pay me any mind when I went along with them. They even let me ride one of the horses they had stolen. Happened to be one of our own horses, too."

Mis' Sally and Thad laughed together. She was able to laugh, not because she was unfeeling about losing her husband and her home, but because she was not the kind to cry about what could not be helped.

"Those Comanches might as well have butchered me right then and there as to take these little ones away from me," she said. "They are all I've got to live for."

After that Thad and Melissa managed to see Mis' Sally occasionally. Even though she was unable to do anything to help them, it was a comfort to have her near. She was someone who knew their own folk.

As summer came on, bands of braves began to leave on foraging expeditions. They traveled toward the east, taking some of their women to do the work of the camp. Thad knew where they were heading, and he got more and more restless as the days passed. Now and then a band of raiders returned. Several prisoners were brought in, but most of them were small children, who were as timid of Thad and Melissa as of their captors. Thad examined every horse they brought in to see if any bore the Branson or the Conway brand. He wondered what outrages the raiders were committing in the region of home.

All summer the captives hoped for rescue or for some opportunity to escape, but they were watched every minute. The summer passed. The days were bright and sunny, but the nights were chill. Every day while he was cutting meat to dry, Thad thought of escape. He would do as Mis' Sally had suggested—escape with Melissa, then tell her sons where Timmy and Tommy and their grandmother could be found.

"They'll make such a cleaning-out of Comanches as no Injun ever thought of," she assured him. "They'll fetch those young ones home again, or my name isn't Sally Buchanan."

She had made several suggestions, and Thad decided to act on one of them. He slipped a little of the meat under his buckskin shirt, and on his way through the village he gave a small piece of it to each dog he met. His hope was to make friends of the dogs so they would not raise an uproar if they met him some night.

When the meat on the racks had dried, he began taking a few strips each day from every rack he could approach without being caught. Although he had been taught that stealing is a sin, he hardly considered this stealing. Rather, this was a means of saving two lives. More than that, he had earned it by forced labor. Melissa was due some of it, too, for she worked as hard as any squaw every day. Thad hoped it would prove a means of keeping them both alive on their journey home.

He dug a little cave in the bank of the stream where the branches of a willow tree hung down over the opening. He lined the little cavity with flat stones and slipped a larger one over the opening. Almost every day he added to the cache of meat with pieces filched from the drying racks. Now and then Melissa was able to bring some honey-and-pecan cakes or some pemmican to add to it.

Their plans were taking definite form now. With Mis' Sally to furnish ideas that only an older person would think of, they felt sure that they would be able to escape.

"But mind, now," Mis' Sally warned them, "don't you let me know when you're leaving. I don't want to know anything about it. I'll know well enough when you've gone."

Thad stopped among the ponies every day on his way to search for wood. Often he would single out Bullet and feed him dried berries and grass. He even gave him a little honey once. Of course, he did not neglect Little-bit, who came running whenever she saw Thad.

Twice Thad sneaked from his bed at night to learn how well the horse herd was guarded, and Bullet and Little-bit came to him the same as ever. It was just as he had thought. A few young braves had been stationed to guard the ponies, but they were sound asleep beside a small fire.

As the fall winds sent tumbleweeds rolling across the country, Thad got another idea. He would choose a night for their escape when the wind was blowing. Then he and Melissa would act like a pair of tumbleweeds. A tumbleweed would roll a little way, pause for some minutes, then roll rapidly again.

Thad had few opportunities to talk with Melissa without arousing suspicion. When he would pass her with Indians nearby, he would murmur, "I'm still thinking," and this served to keep up their spirits.

Early one morning as he dipped his pail into the stream, he heard a twig break behind him, and a hand gently touched his shoulder.

"Thad!" Melissa's voice brought him to his feet in a hurry.

Spotted Boy and the Comanches

She stood close, and in a hurried whisper said, "Thad, it's September, the Comanche Moon, and they're figuring on starting to New Mexico in a few days to trade the horses to the Comancheros. Do you reckon they'll sell Little-bit?"

This came as a shock. Thad knew that the village was expecting to move, but he thought the Indians had already sold or traded all the horses they intended to.

"I don't believe Scar Pony will let them sell Little-bit if he can help it," Thad said. "He loves her. But I'm sure they'll sell Bullet. He's nobody's horse in particular."

Thad had suspected that something was about to happen. Little Rabbit had been having him help her and Blue Flower press dried meat into tight packs and put them into buckskin bags. She had made him take the buffalo robes out of the tepee and shake them and hang them on the bushes, just as ma used to do with the quilts at home. Then she had had them rolled tight and tied with rawhide strings. He had seen other women of the village busy doing the same thing.

"I heard Buffalo Horn telling his woman to get everything ready to move," Melissa said. "That was day before yesterday, but this is the first time I've had a chance to tell you."

"We'd better make our break soon, then." Thad said.

"That was what I was thinking," Melissa agreed.

"If they take Bullet and the other horses that know me, it will be hard to get another one when we try to leave. How about tonight?" Thad felt excited and short of breath at the thought. And he had to admit he was a little afraid, too.

"Mis' Sally stopped me this morning on my way here," Melissa said. "She told me, 'Time you young ones are a-traveling. This village is going to move.'"

"That settles it, then," Thad said. "Mis' Sally knows best. We'll get ready tonight. Do you think you can make it?"

"Of course I'll be ready." Melissa's voice trembled, and Thad wondered if it was from fear or excitement. After all, they would be risking their lives.

Thad hastily pulled his plans together and gave her directions. "Lissy," he said, "we've got jerky and pemmican enough to feed us for almost two weeks if we don't eat it up too fast. I'll try to get some of Little Rabbit's pecans, too."

"I'll try to get some more of the honey-pecan cakes and pemmican," Melissa promised.

"Now don't be afraid," Thad admonished her. "We'll make it all right. Little-bit will get you home if we should get separated. She's found her way more than once."

"How will I know when to leave Buffalo Horn's lodge?" she asked.

Thad had thought of that, too. "I'll just give a little quavering call like a screech owl. Do you know what they sound like?"

"Of course I do," she said. "I've listened to them many a night. I used to be scared when I heard them, but papa told me what they are."

"All right, then, when you hear the screech owl two or three times close together, go to the creek where we have our cache."

"Where will you be?"

"I'll be with the horses. I'll get Bullet and Little-bit and bring them down to the creek."

"What if some of them wake up?" she asked timidly.

"Play like you are a tumbleweed," Thad said. "You know—squat down behind one and pull your robe over your head. Then crawl along easy with it, and stop now and then like a tumbleweed does.

She giggled. "I think I can be a tumbleweed," she said. "And if I'm caught, I'll pretend I am walking in my sleep. I really do walk in my sleep sometimes, and Buffalo Horn and Talking Woman know it. Their name for me is 'Sleep-Walk Girl.'"

"That's a good thing," Thad said. "These Comanches are superstitious about people walking in their sleep. But don't get caught if you can help it."

"Sh-h-h-h," she cautioned as she bent suddenly to the water to fill her jar. "Someone is coming."

Thad rose with his filled pails and started back toward the

village just as a woman and several girls broke through the bushes on the bank above them.

All that day as he worked, Thad thought over their plan for escape. He considered what might happen if they should be caught. He prayed a little as he thought about what they might do to Melissa. Her captors, Buffalo Horn and his woman, seemed to be more cruel than Yellow Cloud and Little Rabbit were to him. He wondered if it was right for him to let her take the chance.

He collected some rawhide strips for tying their robes on their horses. He did not dare take a saddle. There were only a few in the village, for the Comanches generally sold or bartered away those they stole. They preferred to ride with only a blanket or with a saddle of their own making. He had already cached a hackamore and a regular bit-bridle under his buffalo robe in the lodge.

What would happen if they did not get away? How long would it take them to reach home? How would they keep from freezing if there should be a norther? Worst of all, what if the Comanches should catch them? He tried to think of anything he might have forgotten. He believed he had made a pretty good plan and that he had prepared everything well. The attempt should not fail.

Break for Freedom

10

THAD was sure he would get no sleep that night, though he knew he needed the rest. But he was still young, and he was tired. Less than a minute after he had wrapped himself in his buffalo robe, he was sound asleep.

He had feared he would not waken as he had planned, but along in the night something awakened him—the quavering call of a "screech owl." He shook his head and blinked his eyes open. He, Thad, was the one that should have been making that call. Could it be a real screech owl calling outside Yellow Cloud's village at this moment?

It came again. The boy quickly rolled up his old buffalo robe

and got the two bridles from under it. Everything else he needed was hidden in the little cave.

He crept, huddled on his haunches, to the edge of the lodge where he had loosened two of the pegs the night before. His heart was beating like a woodpecker drumming on a tree. Yellow Cloud turned over in his sleep and mumbled something just as Thad was slipping under the edge of the tepee. Thad lay still until heavy breathing inside told him the chief was asleep again.

On hands and knees Thad crawled as fast as he could toward old Buffalo Horn's tepee to signal Melissa. He kept hoping he would not disturb the dogs. He had gone only a little way when a low growl warned him there would soon be a yammering. He spoke softly to the cur and threw it a piece of pemmican. The dog snatched it, sniffed in Thad's direction, then slunk back as though satisfied.

As the boy neared Buffalo Horn's lodge and was about to give another screech owl's call, he heard it again. It came from the direction of the horse herd, and was repeated a minute later. That was Melissa. He knew it was! She had beaten him to it!

Thad felt a little ashamed, yet it made him feel better. She apparently had the needed courage. Thad got to his feet and broke into a run, heading straight for the horse herd. In the pale light of the stars he could barely distinguish their outlines. The guards' fire had died down, and he felt sure the men and boys were asleep. There was nothing to fear from enemies on a night as cold as this, so they had grown careless.

Slipping along the edge of the herd, Thad called softly, "Little-bit, Bullet, come!"

No second call was needed. Two forms broke free from the herd, their hobbles slowing them up. Thad hurried to them, for he was afraid that they would nicker and waken the guards. He crammed some dry grass into their mouths and whispered endearments into their ears. They nuzzled him affectionately. As fast as he could, he slipped the hackamore on Bullet and the bridle on Little-bit. He untied their buckskin hobbles and tied his buffalo robe on the back of Bullet. Then he led the two of them away from the herd. His eyes were getting accustomed to the darkness, and he tried to find open, sandy stretches which would muffle their hoofbeats.

In a little while he saw Melissa, a slender figure against the reflected gleam of the starlight on the creek. He felt easier when he saw her, for he remembered that he should have told her to have the cache of supplies ready for loading. It would have saved time, and time was the important thing now—time to get far away.

Thad handed the reins of the horses to Melissa while he hurried to the hiding place under the willows and took out the provisions. Dividing the jerky, nuts, and pemmican into equal shares, they tied their bundles on their horses.

They led the ponies down the creek under the three-foot banks till they felt they were out of hearing of the village. Their teeth were chattering with nervous excitement. They mounted and Thad gave Melissa some whispered instructions.

"If we hear those Comanches following us and they seem about to catch up with us," he said, "I'll take off in a different direction and circle around so they will follow me. But you keep going toward the east."

"What will become of me if they catch you?" Melissa asked in a worried tone.

"You just stay on Little-bit and keep going. Don't leave her for a minute. Stay with her even when you let her graze at night. Keep her hobbled and hold onto her rope. It is a long one." Thad had brought a rope for staking each horse while it grazed.

"But I might lose the way if you are not with me," she said.

"I reckon *you* might, but Little-bit won't. She has escaped from the Comanches four times and got home every time. You won't even have to guide her. Just give her her head."

There was something else that worried Thad and he cautioned Melissa about it.

"Little-bit's mighty poor, so you'll have to let her graze some every night. Make sure she gets water when she's thirsty, too."

In a few minutes they let the horses pick up speed. Thad felt happy and lighthearted, as their preparations for escape were well thought out. They had had detailed advice from Sally Buchanan, who knew all there was to know about Comanches, Thad believed.

They traveled for an hour at a gallop, stopping now and then to listen for any sound that might indicate they were being followed. It seemed to Thad that Bullet was as eager to get away from Yellow Cloud's village as was Little-bit. They had to be reined down, or they would have galloped at top speed. But Thad did not want them to run themselves out at the beginning. They had a long way to travel.

He pulled Bullet to a walk as the first gray of the coming day could be seen in the east. He listened. No sound reached his ears save the whisper of the wind in the dry grass. The fugitives nibbled pemmican and jerky while they watered the horses at a small stream and let them graze for an hour.

They traveled at a slower speed during the day, stopping at times to listen. At noon they ate a little and drank at another stream. They traveled until the stars came out. With every beat of Bullet's hoofs Thad's heart was saying, "Going home! Going home!"

They hobbled their horses and ate a little supper. Thad tied Bullet's rope around his wrist so the horse would not stray. Then they rolled themselves in their robes and lay down in the shelter of a heap of rocks in a little draw. Dead tired, they slept all night without waking. At daybreak Thad woke to see Melissa rolling out of her robe.

"Thad, Thad!" she was calling. "They're coming!"

Thad listened, and could hear the faraway drumming of hoof-beats. They caught their ponies and mounted. Thad said, "Here, Lissy. Take my share of food. If they catch me, you'll need it and I won't."

They let their horses out to a run, but in less than an hour Thad knew that they were going to be overtaken. "Run for it, Lissy!" he shouted. "I'm taking off toward the left." He saw her face as he turned Bullet's head. She was about to cry.

He turned to the left and rode hard toward the north. As he

pulled away from Lissy he looked back. Little-bit was running toward the east, putting her whole heart into it. Bullet fought the rein for a minute. Then he, too, settled down to a hard run.

After a little Thad could tell that the Comanches had changed their course to match his. It sounded as though there were eight or ten of them. Nothing at that minute could have pleased him more than the knowledge that they were after him instead of Melissa. He was still trying to get away from those yelling devils, but he knew his flight was hopeless.

As the dawn spread, he looked back, and there they were at his heels. One of them was swinging a rope, while several others had arrows nocked, ready to shoot. There were nine of them, all young warriors. He drew Bullet to a halt, thinking it wiser to risk being taken alive than shot.

There was a chance, Thad believed, that Yellow Cloud or Little Rabbit would keep the village people from harming him. These young braves were yelling like fiends, and when he slowed down, they swarmed about him. Some slapped him with their open hands with stinging blows. Others beat him over the head with their rawhide ropes. Finally one swung a doubled rope, bringing it down on Thad's head. He was knocked from his uneasy perch on Bullet's back, and as he hit the ground everything went black.

The Comancheros

11

WHEN Thad came to his senses he was lying on the ground outside the lodge of Yellow Cloud, bruised, sore, and dazed. It did not help much when Talking Woman, wife of Buffalo Horn, came and kicked him in the ribs. In fact, that was what had brought him to consciousness.

"You bad! You go away!" she scolded. "Where Sleep-Walk Girl?"

Thad pretended he did not understand. She scolded for a while, kicked him several times again, then went away.

In a minute or so Little Rabbit took up where Talking Woman had left off. She screamed at Thad for five minutes without letting up. It did not matter much to Thad, for he was not afraid of her so long as she was only scolding. He only half understood what she was saying, she was so angry. He stood before her with what he supposed was a silly grin on his face.

Yellow Cloud came and listened. Thad wondered what the chief had in mind to do to him, but when Little Rabbit had at last run down, he merely grunted and walked away. Little Rabbit handed the water pails to Thad and yelled, "Get water!"

As Thad limped toward the creek for water, Scar Pony walked along beside him, scolding some more. "Where my Blackbird?" he repeated over and over. "Why you steal my horse?"

Thad only grinned at the Indian boy. "I steal *my* horse," was all he would say.

By the time they had reached the creek, Scar Pony's anger had spent itself, and he was challenging Thad to a friendly wrestling match. But Thad had no desire to enter any of the games of the Indian boys just then. All that day Thad worked harder than ever before. Little Rabbit seemed determined to make him sorry for his attempt to return to his own folk. She had tried to make a good Comanche of him. However, the boy was pretty sure that the

Indian's anger would not last long. He also felt sure that the feeling of the men, at least, was to some extent an admiration for his courage and spunk in attempting to escape.

"Spotted Boy Comanche. Not Long Knife boy!" Little Rabbit said several times during the day, as though saying it would make it true.

Thad tried to cover up the fact that he was tired, even though he was near exhaustion. He had found that the easiest way to get along with the Comanches was to obey cheerfully and to take their abuse without flinching.

The next morning when he was sent for wood, Thad went close to the camp of War Hawk's village. He hoped to run across Sally Buchanan. Sure enough, he found her gathering brush and buffalo chips. With her were several Comanche girls and a little white boy, a recent captive, besides her own grandchildren, Timmy and Tommy. She came toward Thad with a big grin on her face.

"Well, Thad, I see you didn't make it."

The boy was feeling pretty glum. All he could do was shake his head. Mis' Sally patted him on the shoulder in a motherly way. "Don't you fret none, honey. You'll get your chance another time. I hear that Melissa got away. Where do you reckon she is by now?"

"She's a far piece down the road, I bet," Thad boasted in his defeat. "She's riding my pony, Little-bit, and you know Little-bit has escaped from these Comanches before. Made it home every time, too."

"Good for Little-bit, then!" Mis' Sally exclaimed. "I do admire a spunky critter, horse or man. The girl will get there all right."

But Thad was not so sure. He wasn't even sure Mis' Sally felt as certain as she pretended.

"Do you think she will?" he asked.

"Why, of course she'll make it, son," she said confidently. "She's got plenty to eat, and there's water along the way. Did she have a buffalo robe?"

Thad nodded.

"Then she'll make it home without a doubt."

Spotted Boy and the Comanches

She changed the subject then. "We're starting to move to-morrow," she reminded him. "I hear Yellow Cloud's braves will be heading for New Mexico. I reckon they'll take you along to help herd horses. I don't know when I'll see you again."

Thad bade her good-bye and turned to go. But she called him back.

"Now, Thad," she said, "I'm an old woman and I may not live to take these young ones home to their people. But I don't aim for them to grow up Comanches. I'd like to hear you promise that when you do get home again—and I'm satisfied your prayers will be answered as to that—you will tell my sons where these boys are. Most likely they'd have torn up the country looking for us, but they don't even know we're alive. Will you promise you'll help them locate these little fellows, Thad?"

The Comancheros' entire business was trading with Indian tribes.

"I sure will, Mis' Sally," Thad promised. "But I don't reckon I'll need to. You'll most likely be home by the time I get there."

"There's one more thing, Thad." Mis' Sally was more serious than he had ever seen her.

"This young one," she said, indicating the small captive boy, "all he can tell us is that his name is Willy. I can't for the life of me find out where he came from, and those red devils aren't about to tell me. If you could help find his people, there would be one less white boy growing up to be a Comanche brave."

Thad looked the little fellow over. The youngster clung to Mis' Sally's ragged doeskin robe and looked up at him with big blue eyes. It would be a shame for him never to be found by white folk. Thad promised to report the boy if he himself ever reached home.

"I reckon a woman of my age ought to be ashamed of herself

No questions were asked about where the Indians got their horses.

if she hasn't got as much faith in the Lord's protection as a boy," said Mis' Sally.

Thad grinned. "I reckon the Lord's got as good reason to save you from the Comanches as he has me. I'll see you at the Double Bar O Ranch next meeting time."

Mis' Sally whooped at that. Then she stuck out her bony, weathered hand. "Put her there, Thad! I'll see you then, and the little ones will be with me."

As he walked away, Thad wondered how long it would be. But his confidence had been restored in talking to Mis' Sally, and that helped a great deal.

War Hawk gathered his people to take them north to the reservation. September had come and he would make a leisurely passage, arriving in Indian Territory before cold weather set in. He was sending a band of his braves with their squaws to drive his trade horses to New Mexico. They would accompany Yellow Cloud's young men and horses.

A day or so later Yellow Cloud gave orders as to who should accompany him on the journey westward. Little Rabbit would go, but Blue Flower would remain behind with the baby. Thad would go, and he was given Bullet to ride. He was to help in driving the bands of horses. There were nearly a thousand horses to sell, the result of a summer's thievery. Thad was glad Little-bit was beyond their reach, for she also might be sold, in spite of Scar Pony's desires.

The families, with their goods packed on travois pulled by horses, walked or rode a half mile to windward of the herd. But Thad, riding alongside the horses, was often choked with dust stirred up by the animals. He realized he was traveling farther and farther from his home. For days and weeks they journeyed toward the west and a little southwest. He was about as gloomy and hopeless as he had ever been in his life, despite Scar Pony's renewed friendliness. So hopeless did he feel, that his mind could devise no plan for escape. He was becoming resigned to living with these people who, for all their savagery, had their good qualities, too. He had come to the place where he felt he might be living with them the rest of his life.

*   *   *

They spent several weeks trading with the Comancheros. Thad had heard of the Comancheros all his life, and had thought of them as strange outlanders. But he found most of them to be simple Mexican people. A scattering among them were renegade French, Spanish, American, and half-breeds. They lived in little adobe houses, and their villages might have been taken for ordinary settlements of Rio Grande Mexicans, had it not been for their large warehouses and enormous corrals. Their entire business was trading with Indian tribes. They also traded with the Apaches, but most of their trading was with Comanches. No questions were asked as to where the Indians had gotten their horses and equipment.

Thad had heard that these Comancheros were the real cause of the white settlers' troubles. He had heard Johnny Ainsworth say, "I do believe the government could bring the Comanches under control if they didn't have that bunch of traders to receive the stolen goods."

Thad could see the sense in Mr. Johnny's statement. He saw hundreds of horses bartered to the Comancheros for guns, ammunition, and beads. There were also woolen blankets and hand-crafted jewelry of turquoise and silver from the Pueblos and the Navajos.

No time was lost by the Comancheros in disposing of the horses they had taken in trade, especially those that wore brands. These were sent immediately into Chihuahua or westward to the Apache Indians.

After two weeks Yellow Cloud had finished his trading, keeping only enough horses to mount his band and to carry the goods received in trade. They had packed camp and were on their way back toward their old location, when a battle with some Mexicans briefly delayed them.

Some of Yellow Cloud's braves and a few of War Hawk's double-dealing young Comanches had lingered behind the others and had stolen back some of the horses they had just sold to the Comancheros. They drove them as fast as they could to join the herd of the traveling band. Yellow Cloud kept scouts out in the direction of Morada in the event the Mexicans should try to surprise his band.

One day a scout came pounding into camp. "The Comancheros come!" he announced.

"How many?" Yellow Cloud asked.

"A large band," the scout answered. "All armed with carbines. Very angry. On good horses, they come fast."

The camp was in a turmoil. Yellow Cloud and his warriors arrayed themselves and their horses for battle. Faces and bodies were painted. Strips of bright calico, red flannel, ribbons, and feathers were woven into horses' manes and tails. Yellow Cloud put on strings of beads, a large necklace of bear claws, and a man's gold watch on a heavy chain.

Next Thad saw him fasten around his neck a thin strip of rawhide from which hung a cameo brooch. A letter "M" was worked into the design of the gold border. Thad had seen that locket before. It had been Marcella Branson's! The boy had almost come to like old Yellow Cloud and resign himself to adopting Comanche ways, but now he knew he could never look at him again without thinking of that cameo pin and what it meant.

The braves rode to battle, not returning till the next morning. They had killed several of the Mexicans, and also brought their own dead. Thad felt pretty bad about a prisoner they brought in now. The poor captive seemed half dead, but that did not rouse feelings of pity in the hearts of his captors, who promptly began to abuse him.

After a while he heard the sound of many horses followed by an outcry from Yellow Cloud's people. The Mexicans were returning with reinforcements.

The battle did not last long. The Mexicans had come back to rescue their friend who had been taken in the previous battle. Thad found himself praying for the enemy's success. When at last the Comancheros galloped away, they had the rescued prisoner with them.

Thad was almost as happy about the outcome of the battle as he would have been over his own release from the Comanches. For a little while he even considered running away with the rescuers and throwing himself upon the mercy of the Mexicans. But that would only take him farther from his own home. Besides, he *knew* the sort of peril he faced with the Comanches. He did not know what might happen to him with the Comancheros. It might only be exchanging a lesser peril for a greater.

Battle With Rangers

12

BY THE time the band of horse traders had reached the old village camp, it was mid-October, a year since Thad's kidnapping from home. After seeing with his own eyes how cruel his captors could be, he found it difficult to feel as friendly toward them as before.

He tried to keep in mind what Johnny Ainsworth had said about hating Comanches! "The Comanches are living their lives as they have been raised to live them." But for the present Thad was tired, and he missed the encouraging visits with Mis' Sally Buchanan. He supposed everyone lived his life as he had been taught to live it, but he did not like the way the Comanches had been taught to live theirs.

Thad had one big worry: What had happened to Melissa and Little-bit? He could call to mind every incident of their escape, and he could hear again the hoofbeats of Little-bit fading out toward the sunrise. Had they made it home? Where were they now? Would his brothers know where he was and come in search of him? Those questions went around and around in his brain. If anything had happened to Melissa, he felt, it was his fault for getting her started on such a dangerous journey.

The camp was soon on the move toward the north. As the days went by, he walked for hour after hour in the dust of the moving village, along with some Indian women and children. So many of the horses had been traded off that there were not enough for all to ride. Thad was generally too tired and cold and miserable to think of anything—even home or loved ones. He could not even hope or pray when night came. When he dropped with his smelly old robe wrapped around him, he immediately fell into a deep sleep.

At evening when the band stopped, Thad was dispatched to gather wood for the cook fires. Then he helped Little Rabbit set up Yellow Cloud's tepee. That meant dragging the lodgepoles from the sides of the poor, tired ponies and unrolling the heavy buffalo-hide cover from the travois.

Thad carried his robe strapped across his shoulders. It was his only possession. He sometimes worried about his appearance, imagining it to be that of a neglected, weather-beaten scarecrow. He thought of his ragged buckskin, his face streaked with dirt, his hair a thatch of dirty straw. He felt pretty sorry for himself sometimes. The fact was, he was beginning to feel like a Comanche youngster himself, and he disliked the idea.

Finally Yellow Cloud decided to give the village a chance to rest and find some meat. It became bitterly cold as a norther swept down across the plains and whistled around the camp all of one day and night. Thad thought longingly of the snug front room at home where the family gathered to sit out the northers. They would crack pecans, play dominoes, and tell stories. He thought he would die of homesickness.

One day a band of young hunters returned to camp leading ponies loaded with buffalo and antelope meat. The camp was full of noise and excitement as they came galloping in, with old women screaming, children shouting, and dogs barking. Anyone who thinks of Indians as the strong, silent type should visit a Comanche village when there is excitement afoot.

But the hunters brought news that stirred up more excitement than the meat did.

"We saw Long Knives," Two Lances reported. The elders began to question him, while Thad, Scar Pony, and the other boys listened.

"How many Long Knives?" Buffalo Horn wanted to know.

Two Lances held up his hands with fingers spread, dropped them, and raised them again, until he had indicated thirty.

"Did you give them battle?" Yellow Cloud asked.

"No, they were too many. They had many guns and wanted to parley. We did not wish battle. We were too few and we had come to hunt."

"For what did they wish to parley?" Yellow Cloud asked.

109

"They were hunting buffalo as we were," Two Lances explained. "But they wanted to ask us if we had seen a white boy and girl that Comanches took many moons ago."

"What did you tell them?"

"We told them we knew of no white boy or girl in any Comanche camp."

It suddenly struck Thad that he was the boy and Melissa the girl the Long Knives were asking about. Then he realized what that meant. If the men were inquiring for both a boy and a girl, then Melissa and Little-bit had never reached home. They had had plenty of time—months. If they were not at home by this time, they were either dead or had been captured by some other band of Indians. Perhaps they had even been captured by another tribe.

Thad was more discouraged than ever. As they traveled each day toward Indian Territory and he realized that they were getting farther and farther from his home, he would awake in the night and cry. He even quit saying his prayers.

One night another norther blew down on them, howling, screaming, and moaning, and bringing a bitter, piercing cold. Thad lay
in his buffalo robe with his teeth chattering. The mournful wind
seemed to him to be sorrowing for his loved ones.

Perhaps the sorrow was for Melissa, too, Thad thought. If she
and Little-bit had not reached home, some terrible thing must have
happened to them. Did they get lost? Did she die of exposure?
Maybe some of Yellow Cloud's braves had killed her. But where,
then, was Little-bit? If the people of this village had taken Little-bit
again, they would have brought her back. But she had never
appeared among the ponies of the herd since Melissa rode away
on her. Scar Pony had boasted that he would bring back his Blackbird, but he had never done it.

The morning after the norther struck, rain and sleet began. It
whipped about the camp, drenching the people, even cutting their
skin. The ponies huddled together with their tails to the wind.

Spotted Boy and the Comanches

Thad was sure he would have died in that storm had he not been kept active fetching wood and helping feed the fires.

At last the storm blew itself out. The sun came forth, shining on a white and frozen world.

*   *   *

Thad was gathering wood early one morning when he heard the pounding of hoofs. A mounted brave splashed through the water a little way from him. He recognized the rider as Mad Raven, a member of a small hunting party that had gone in search of meat. A scout had located a small herd of buffalo only a few miles from the camp.

Mad Raven's horse was lathered, and bloody foam blew in flecks from his mouth. Something was up. What had the hunters run into? Thad hurried to gather his load of wood and started back toward camp. He wondered if the hunters had run into white men again. He hoped fervently that they had.

Scar Pony, Running Fox, Boy Who Laughs, and Small Weasel joined Thad as he hurried toward Yellow Cloud's lodge. They would stay as near the council fire as they dared, to listen to the news. They soon had the gist of it.

"Our braves fight with Long Knives," Running Fox said. The women and girls behind them broke into scornful laughter at this. A girl threw a stone that hit Thad in the back. Another ran up and spit at him. Thad paid no heed.

"Our braves kill many Long Knives," Small Weasel boasted. "White men run away."

Thad was pretty sure Small Weasel knew as little as he did about it, so he tried a little boasting of his own. "White men do not run away—ever!" he said.

Scar Pony said quietly, "We have not heard what happened. We know only that there was a battle."

Thad listened attentively as the story was told from the beginning. "Medicine Dog shot at a buffalo," Mad Raven was saying. "He missed and fired two more times. Our other men shot arrows at the bull. I was a long way from where Medicine Dog was.

The Long Knives heard the shots. They came on their horses, running."

"The same white men you saw ten suns ago?" Yellow Cloud asked.

Mad Raven hesitated. "I think maybe some are the same," he said.

"Were the white men settlers or Rangers?"

"I think some settlers, some Rangers. Some rode all together like soldiers, only they do not have 'U.S.' on their saddles, like soldiers." He drew the letters in the sand.

Yellow Cloud nodded emphatically. "They are Rangers. How many do you think?"

"Maybe ten settlers—thirty Rangers."

Yellow Cloud and the other men made a clucking noise with their tongues.

"We go help our hunters," Yellow Cloud snapped.

At a sign from him the braves hurried from the lodge to get their weapons. A few minutes later they pounded out of the village on their horses, armed to the teeth and stripped and painted for battle. There were about sixty of them. Only Yellow Cloud and Buffalo Horn wore the war bonnets of eagle feathers. Yellow Cloud's hung down to his horse's back.

Thad was dazed. A few miles away were his own people. Maybe they were not his own brothers, but at least they were folk who might take him to his home. He tried to think. If he could only sneak away, he might be able to reach the white men.

But Little Rabbit was one jump ahead of him. She seized him by the shoulder and snapped at him, "You, Spotted Boy, you no run away. You work!"

She set him to work helping break camp, for they were getting ready to travel again. Thad worked automatically while his mind went around and around. Over and over he prayed, "O Lord, help our people to win!"

Yellow Cloud's tepee was the last in the village to come down. Thad was helping Little Rabbit roll the hide cover of it when the

113

sounds of battle reached their ears: faraway shots, Indian yells, an occasional shout from the white men.

Thad was bursting with excitement. Was his release at hand? Suddenly the sounds increased in volume. The beating of hoofs became louder as the warriors were driven back to the village. White men were yelling now, too.

"They're winning! They're winning! Our men are winning!" Thad yelled in Comanche, jumping up and down.

Suddenly he was seized from behind. A hand was clapped over his mouth and a cloth gag stuffed into it and fastened. His hands and feet were bound. He was pushed under a heap of buffalo robes that lay beside the pile of lodgepoles and the rolled-up cover of Yellow Cloud's tepee.

He fought and kicked against his fetters, but he was so tightly bound that he could scarcely move. He gagged over the wad of cloth, and was unable to bring a sound from his throat.

He finally concluded that the best thing to do was to lie still. Surely, he thought, if the white men took the village, they would look under every pile of robes. Then something plumped down upon him. It felt like a person sitting on the robes that covered him. He learned later that it was a very old woman who looked as though her rickety bones might fall apart any moment.

The sounds of battle came nearer until they were in the village all around him. The firing ceased, but he could hear men's voices, white men's voices! He tried to yell, to make some sort of noise, but it was no use.

He thought, "They are searching the village. Surely they will find me!" He wondered if Reed or Giles or Mr. Johnny Ainsworth were among them.

He lost consciousness then from lack of air. The next thing he knew he was being hauled roughly from the heap of robes. The Comanches had relied on the mercy of the white men not to disturb an apparently sick old woman. The Comanches had never been known to spare anyone because of age or helplessness in their raids on the whites, but they knew the white men were different, and had taken advantage of this to keep Thad a prisoner.

As the boy gradually returned to his senses, everything in the village was in tumult. Wailing for the dead had begun. Heaps of family possessions were scattered, and women and children were gathering them together. Thad knew that the white men had turned them over in their search for him. Many of the horses had been shot or driven away.

A feeling of bitter sorrow was in the air. Thad wondered how the defeat of his captors would affect their treatment of him. Since his attempted escape, he had been treated with a measure of respect and friendliness, for the Indians admired a person with spunk and courage.

This was one of the saddest days of the boy's captivity. That morning he had believed himself in the hands of friends. Now he found himself in the most serious danger of his life. As he sat on the ground trying to recover from the near-suffocation, he was kicked by almost every villager, man or woman, who passed by. The children hissed at him, and the boys and girls his own age spit upon him—all but Scar Pony, Boy Who Laughs, and Running Fox. They stayed away. He was sore at heart and broken in spirit.

As the days passed, the villagers disposed of their dead, with mourning and wailing. Thad tried to tell himself, "Serves them right," but somehow he felt himself grieving with them. He had known several of the young warriors who had been killed in battle, and he was sorry about them. He could not find it in his heart to hate them now, regardless of what they had done to him.

Eight of the warriors had been killed and a number of horses had been driven away. The horses that remained were loaded to the limit. To Thad and to every woman and girl an extra burden was given to carry. Travel was slow and the skies were gray. As they neared their destination, a steady drizzle fell.

Scar Pony often walked beside Thad. Scar Pony seemed to sense Thad's keen disappointment and sympathized with him. He said, "Maybe you find your people when we get to the agency."

Thad had no idea what the agency was like.

"Where is the agency?" he asked.

"Where we are going," Scar Pony answered. "It is in Indian Territory not far from Fort Sill."

Thad had often heard of Fort Sill and of Indian Territory, but he knew little about them. Nor did he know anything of the location of Fort Sill. It did comfort him to have Scar Pony show himself friendly.

Thad was sick the last few days of their journey. He had pneumonia, and no wonder, after the exposure of the past few weeks. His chest hurt, his head ached, and he burned with fever. It seemed as though each time he coughed, something tore loose inside him. The thought of food gagged him.

Little Rabbit put an old woollen shirt on him. Some poor settler had doubtless yielded his life with that shirt, but the boy was too ill to think of that.

It did not occur to Thad to wonder why she should show so much interest in his getting well. Looking back after many years, he came to believe that Little Rabbit was attached to him with a motherly sort of affection. He knew she had lost two sons in battle, one against the white soldiers and one against the Apaches in New Mexico.

As Thad stumbled along, Scar Pony took his hand and placed it on his own shoulder. Tears glittered in his dark eyes as he looked at the white boy.

"Lean on me," he said. "Scar Pony is your friend."

A warm surge of gratitude and even love swept through Thad. He knew he would never forget Scar Pony's kindness.

That night Little Rabbit covered Thad with robes until he was weighted down. He was so hot beneath them that he thought he could not bear it. But during the night Little Rabbit came now and then to tuck the covers about him. Just before daylight he broke into a profuse sweat. It left him weak, but his fever seemed to be broken.

Little Rabbit doused him with a bucket of cold water. It took his breath, but then she rubbed him briskly with a scrap of dry hide until he tingled with warmth again. It was drastic treatment, but it seemed to work. He felt better than he had for a long time, although he was still weak and shaky.

Little Rabbit brought him a bowl of steaming broth. "Drink!" she ordered. "The broth of antelope will make you strong. The heat will warm you."

Thad was as hungry as a mother wolf now. His ribs stuck out almost like barrel staves, and he shook so that he could hardly hold the cup. But the hot brew seemed to pour warmth and strength into him.

Scar Pony walked beside him again that last day and made him lean on his shoulder. Little Rabbit and Blue Flower could not do enough for him. Even Yellow Cloud came—to feel his bones and mutter something about meatless ribs.

Thad was beginning to feel affection toward these enemies of his people. Scar Pony and Little Rabbit had made his lot as easy as they were able, especially in these last weeks. The people of the village, he thought, might be compared to an assortment of white people. Some were good, some cruel, some indifferent.

He kept remembering Mr. Johnny's words, "They live as they have been raised to live." He let that speak for itself.

At the Agency

13

"**W**HEN will we get to Indian Territory?" Thad asked Scar Pony. The people of Yellow Cloud's band were setting up camp, and it seemed to be on a more permanent basis than usual.

Scar Pony laughed. "We are in Indian Territory since three suns."

"But where is Fort Sill? Where is the agency?" Thad wanted to know.

"My father and Yellow Cloud have gone to the agency to get flour and sugar and beef," Scar Pony said. "It is not far, maybe two hours. They will be back before the sun is gone."

Thad's hopes fell. He had hoped they would camp near the agency. If there were white people there, they would know that no Indian had hair as white as his or face splashed with freckles. Little Rabbit's walnut stain had worn off. He made up his mind that somehow he would show himself at the agency. But he would have to wait until he gained strength.

On good days the people of Yellow Cloud's village got together with those of other Comanche bands on the reservation. They had a hilarious time talking over happenings since they had last met. They gambled, danced, played games, and staged contests of strength and endurance. They did a lot of horse racing, too. Thad recognized some braves from the band of War Hawk, and learned that their camp was no more than two miles away. He resolved that he would see Mis' Sally at the first opportunity. She always inspired him with hope and courage, and he felt greatly in need of both.

He watched all the horses of the braves that came to their village to see if he could spot one with the Conway Double Bar O brand. If there were any horses with that brand, he would know that the home corrals had been raided.

There were few good days that winter. Snow flew almost every day for weeks, and Thad could not venture out on his own. He coughed most of every night. His appetite was poor, and he had only enough strength to do a few small chores. Little Rabbit was not treating him like a girl anymore, but like a son.

Signs of spring began to appear in March. Redbirds bustled about in the melting snow. Bluebirds began their calling, sweet and sad. Early wild flowers began to push up through the springing grass.

One day two white men rode into the village and talked to Yellow Cloud. When he saw them, Thad started to walk out to where they might see him.

"Go to Blue Flower's lodge!" Little Rabbit ordered sharply, and he knew he must obey.

They stayed but a few moments. That night Thad heard Yellow Cloud talking to the village elders beside the fire.

"Those white men," he was saying, "they come to ask if we are satisfied with what the agency does for us."

One of the old men answered in grumbling tones, "They give us beef and beans, flour and bacon. But we want our own hunting grounds back that these Long Knives took from us."

Another laughed and said, "Our hunting grounds are better than before the white settlers came. They raise beef for us and horses to trade to the Comancheros."

Another said with a chuckle, "Government feeds us in the winter, and we raid the ranches in summer. It is better for us this way. We no longer hunger in summer or in winter."

"These men at the agency—they are like children," one remarked. The others laughed as he went on, "We butcher their horses and their beef. We even kill their servants and they do nothing. They are weak. They are afraid of us."

Thad thought that if what they were saying was true, there would be little point in going to them for help. Then he remembered how boastful the Indians were, and stayed by his decision to show himself at the agency. The trouble was that he had not the slightest idea where the agency was. And he was still feeling as weak as a kitten.

The next morning he spoke to Scar Pony, who had made at least one trip to the agency with his father.

"Can you tell me how to get to the agency?" he asked the Indian boy.

"You want to go to the agency?"

"Yes, I must find my people." Thad thought he might as well tell the truth.

Scar Pony nodded understandingly and looked around him to see if anyone else was near. Then he stooped and drew a sort of map on the ground with a stick, explaining each landmark on the way.

When Thad had memorized the map carefully, he erased it by dragging a twig with dry leaves across it.

When Thad awoke the next morning, he crawled to the edge of the tepee and discovered that it was snowing again. Big flakes fell thick upon a landscape that was already white. He started out to follow Scar Pony's directions, but he had gone only a little way when he knew that he would become hopelessly lost in the snow. So he crept back to his buffalo robe to wait for a better day.

Two days later he was able to trudge away from the camp. He headed in the direction of War Hawk's village, hoping he might run across Mis' Sally and talk to her. He wanted her cheerful comfort and hoped she might have an idea as to how he could present himself at the agency.

He had tried to find Mis' Sally before but had not been able. This morning he saw her a short way off, coming toward him, trying to keep from being seen by those at War Hawk's camp.

"Well, howdy, Thad!" she greeted him in her cheerful way.

"Howdy, Mis' Sally!" he said.

"Son, I've been trying to see you ever since I heard that Yellow Cloud had come this way. Now I've got something to tell you. I started out this morning with my mind made up that I'd see you or get my hair lifted in the trying."

She looked Thad over and her expression changed.

"Law, son, what have they been doing to you? You're as poor as a snake. I never in my life saw such a rack of bones supposed to be alive."

"I've been sick," Thad told her. "But what was it you wanted to tell me?"

"Oh, yes. I've got some news that I reckon might interest you. There were some soldiers from the fort' who came along one morning when I was getting water. They were surprised to see a poor old white woman among a passel of Comanches. Those soldiers asked me a lot of questions, and then their officer asked me some more when he came up to us. He asked me how I came to be with the Comanches. When I told him how I just naturally joined up with them, he laughed fit to kill. I told him about my grandsons and about you, Thad."

The boy was choking with excitement at this. "What did they say, then?" he asked her.

"They didn't have much to say about us, son. But I reckon they'll pass the word along. The main thing I wanted to tell you about is what the Tonkawas told me. There were two Tonkawa scouts with the soldiers. They said that in one of their villages there was a white girl. She had been with them for over a year. Some of their hunters found her wandering on the prairie half dead, and out of her mind, too, I reckon. She was riding a black pony."

"Little-bit and Melissa!" Thad exclaimed. "Where is their village?"

"Those Tonkawas were working as scouts for the army and I guess their village is somewhere in Texas. I couldn't make head or tail of what they were trying to tell me about the location. It wasn't their own village. They called the chief Willowbird, I believe. I don't understand Tonkawa talk too well. The officers said they'd try to find out more about it. Anyway, by this time the village is most likely moved from where it was."

Several mornings later Thad awoke to find Little Rabbit looking at him. There was something in her gaze that reminded him of the way his mother looked when she used to waken him in the morning, and it brought a warm feeling to his heart.

He had felt sort of affectionate toward Little Rabbit before, especially when she sat with the other women, doing what she loved best—working designs in beads on bags of antelope hide or doeskin. At such times she reminded him of his own mother, who would sit on an afternoon crocheting, knitting, or making quilts with bright pieces of calico.

Little Rabbit was holding something in her hand. Thad got to his feet.

"Put them on!" she said. It was a suit of fine buckskin, carefully made. It was fringed at the yoke and sleeve seams, and heavily embroidered across the breast, at the wrists, and along the seams of the leggings.

Thad was amazed. It was one of the most beautiful suits he had ever seen.

"For me?" he asked in surprise.

"Put them on!" she repeated.

Thad dressed himself. The suit fitted him quite well, though it was a little loose because he was so thin. Little Rabbit gave him a pair of moccasins. For the first time in months he was not ashamed of his appearance. These were the dress clothes of a young brave. White men's feet are generally larger than an Indian's, and the white men of Texas grow tall. So he judged that these garments had belonged to someone older than himself. They were fancy feathers for a slave in an Indian camp, and he glowed with pride as he looked at Little Rabbit and tried to thank her.

"You made these, Little Rabbit?"

She nodded.

"You made them for me?"

"You wear. They are for you. One time belong to my son, Eagle Wing. Now he need them no more."

Thad's feelings were mixed. He was supposed to hate these people—at least he supposed he should. They were supposed to hate him, too, for his people had killed some of theirs. Yet Little

Rabbit had given him a suit that had belonged to a dearly loved son who had fought gallantly, but had fallen before the guns of the Long Knives.

As he tried to give her his thanks, he noticed a brightness in Little Rabbit's eyes. He was sure it was a glistening tear. He wondered how much of her grief was for her own son and how much for the white boy.

"You go today," she said. "Yellow Cloud takes you to the agency. Go to your people."

Thad could hardly believe she meant what she was saying. He ran to tell Scar Pony.

"They are very kind," he said. "They are sending me to my people."

Scar Pony smiled. "Yellow Cloud knows that the white soldiers know you are here. He knows they will come and find you and punish us. This way he will sell you and get money or blankets."

Scar Pony, turning serious eyes on the white boy, said, "My Blackbird, I give her to you. If you find her, she is yours. I will never take her from you again." Sadness shone in the dark eyes, and Thad, too, felt grief at the parting.

"Why do you do this for me, Scar Pony?" he asked.

"You are my friend," Scar Pony said solemnly. "I wish I might see you again. But that cannot be."

When he was getting ready to ride away with Yellow Cloud, Little Rabbit adjusted the seams and belt of his fine new suit. He knew it was a woman's way of showing affection. He almost expected her to say, as ma would have said, "Now be a good boy!"

Impulsively he reached over and kissed her brown cheek. Little Rabbit was surprised, but she only smoothed his long braids and said, "Sometime, maybe, see again, Spotted Boy." It was a hope he now shared with her.

Thad was dazed as he rode beside Yellow Cloud. There were others with them, but his thoughts kept running ahead. Without a doubt, he told himself, his brothers or his father had been to the agency to look for him, even though the agency was more than

Spotted Boy and the Comanches

three hundred miles from home. Possibly they would be waiting for him there.

Apparently Yellow Cloud had already talked to the man at the agency. He made Thad stop a little distance from the buildings. A man and a woman stood waiting for him, but they were looking at Thad. As Yellow Cloud talked with them, Thad could see that he was wrangling in the typical Indian manner. He felt sure they were haggling over the price.

The white man, heavyset, with a short, dark beard, walked to

Yellow Cloud haggled with the Barnetts over the price for Thad.

where Thad was sitting on the horse. He looked the boy over carefully and said to Yellow Cloud, "Fifty dollars. That is all."

Yellow Cloud shook his head and snarled.

"Fifty-five dollars. That is enough," said the man.

"His people will pay more than that for him," Yellow Cloud argued, in the tone he would have used in speaking to a dog.

"Seventy dollars, then," the man said. "That is all. I will have to feed him until his people find him. Maybe they will never find him."

Yellow Cloud commented as he took the money, "Spotted Boy work good." Thad felt like a mule being examined and haggled over, and that was about what it amounted to.

Yellow Cloud spat at the man's feet, barely missing them. He took hold of the reins of the horse Thad had been riding and rode away. He sat stiff in the saddle, his head high. He gave no backward glance.

The woman came toward Thad. She was dark-haired, red-cheeked, and plump. She wore a gray dress and bonnet, and a snowy-white apron. Thad stood speechless. He had been hungry for the sight of his own kind of people for a long time.

His new owners, Mr. and Mrs. Barnett, were Quakers. As they neared the house, Thad smelled the spicy odor of baking bread. He felt as though he were in heaven. If his feet touched the ground, he was scarcely aware of it.

Mrs. Barnett took Thad to the kitchen while her husband went back into the trading post. In one corner stood a big cookstove, on which bubbled a pot of stew.

"Poor boy," Mrs. Barnett said. "Thee must be starved for white folks' cooking. Sit right down here and eat some cookies and drink this cold milk. That will stay thy stomach until dinnertime." At first Thad found it hard to follow what she was saying. Instead of saying "you" and "yours," she spoke in the language of the Bible and said "thee" and "thine."

One of the easiest things he ever did was to eat the cookies and drink the milk. This was a queer way to treat a bought-and-paid-for slave, Thad thought. But he liked it.

Spotted Boy and the Comanches

"What a puny-looking boy thou art!" Mrs. Barnett exclaimed as she watched him wolfing the cookies and milk. "Didn't those savages feed thee?"

Gulping down a mouthful, Thad stopped eating for a minute and explained. "I have been sick, awful sick. I like to have died."

"Oh," she said. "It's a wonder thee did not die."

But when he told her how Little Rabbit had heaped robes on him to make him sweat and then had doused him with water, and how she had sat beside him most of one night and had made hot broth for him, she looked thoughtful.

"I suppose Little Rabbit did the best for thee that she knew how. We came to this agency from Pennsylvania to help these savages learn how to live like Christians should. But sometimes it is almost more than we can bear, the way they sneer at us and steal our cattle. They have even murdered some of our helpers. They think we are weak because we do not strike back. The Comanches are the worst of the tribes."

In a few weeks the winds of spring had melted the snows and set the field larks to whistling in the willows. The bittersweet scent of wild plum blossoms made Thad ache to go prowling among the shadows of the old creek bottom at home. It was the first day of April, Mrs. Barnett told him. Thad recalled that he had had a birthday back in December. He was fourteen years old.

"Fourteen years old!" He strutted a little when he said it. Now he was almost a man. His legs were long and skinny. His hands and feet were big and bony, and put him in mind of when his dog Whizzer was a pup. Pa had looked at the pup's big, clumsy paws and said, "That pup will make a big dog, mark my words." And he was right. Whizzer grew to be as big as a calf.

Thad spread his hands before Mrs. Barnett. "I expect I'll make a big man. You reckon?"

She smiled at him. "I reckon," she said, imitating his frontier speech.

Thad worked hard, for he felt that he must pay back the $70 Mr. Barnett had paid for him. Though he was happier than at any time since he had been captured by Two Lances, he longed to hear from his people. At times he recalled the voice he had heard among the rocks, assuring him of God's care, and he felt more cheerful.

No doubt God cared for Melissa, too, he thought. When he spoke of it to Mrs. Barnett, she said, "Thou art fortunate thy father made thee learn the Scripture so that the Lord hath called the words to thy mind."

The Quakers and other Christian missionaries were trying to civilize and Christianize the Indian tribes by being friendly toward them. Some of the tribes were responding, and seemed glad to bury the hatchet. They sent their children to the mission schools so they might learn messages from the books with leaves that talked. The Comanches, however, did not understand such a generous spirit—not yet, anyway.

Thad saw two Rangers talking with Mr. Barnett.
"Giles!" he yelled throwing himself at one man.

His Own Kind of People 14

"HAS anyone ever come here to ask about me?" Thad asked Mrs. Barnett that first morning.

"Mr. Barnett will tell thee about that when he comes to dinner," she said. She looked at his buckskin suit.

"Did Little Rabbit make it for thee?" she asked.

"No, ma'am," he replied. "Not for me. She made it for her son, Eagle Wing, but he was killed in a battle with white folk. She gave it to me this morning."

"That was a kind thing for her to do," she said. "I suppose thee would rather look like a white boy, though, would thee not?"

"Yes'm, I reckon I would," Thad answered. Actually, he was just a little proud of that beautiful buckskin suit. He had seen the braves strut in such ornamented suits, and he felt like doing a little strutting himself. In spite of Comanche meanness, he had come near to being an Indian himself.

Mrs. Barnett brought some clothes. She tried them until she found some that would come close to fitting the boy. "These were sent from a Sunday school in the East, for us to distribute to the Indians," she explained. "Now I'll go in the other room and give thee a chance to bathe."

When he had scrubbed himself, Thad got into the underwear, shirt, and breeches she had brought him. Then Mrs. Barnett washed his long hair, clucking over the feathers Little Rabbit had given him along with the buckskin suit. Then she cut it off square below his ears and across his forehead. He looked for all the world like a Dutch boy, but he felt better and cleaner than he had in a long time."

At the dinner table Mrs. Barnett told her husband, "Mr. Barnett, we must put some fat on this boy. His own folk will not recognize him like this."

Again Thad put the question about his people. Surely someone had inquired for him or Melissa.

129

Spotted Boy and the Comanches

Mr. Barnett was a slow-talking man. Thad thought to himself that the man would never get around to saying what he so much wanted to hear.

"Well, there have been several people in the last year inquiring about children. Whether any of them were of thy family or not, I cannot say." He ate a few more mouthfuls while Thad fidgeted. Then he said, "Last August two men—no, it was a man and a boy about fifteen years old, came. They asked about a girl thirteen years old and a boy, fourteen."

"What did they say the girl looked like?" Thad asked breathlessly.

"Black hair, blue eyes, and fair skin. The boy was white-haired and freckle-faced. There are a great many towheaded, freckle-faced boys," he commented, looking at Thad from under his brows.

"They told me the girl was stolen a year ago last summer, along with a little sister. They found the sister dead. They've never heard of the other one."

"Was the girl's name Melissa Branson?" Thad asked.

"Melissa? Yes, I believe that was the name." Mr. Barnett fished into his pocket and brought out a little book. Turning its pages slowly, he finally stopped at one.

"Yes, it was Melissa," he said, "Melissa Branson. The man's name was Wiley Branson, and the boy's, Beauford. The father called him 'Beau.'" He peered at Thad again over his steel-rimmed spectacles. "Has thee ever heard of them?"

"I'm the white-headed boy!" exclaimed Thad. "I know the Bransons. I tried to help Melissa get away from the Comanches, and they caught me. I guess she never got home, if they were still looking for her in August.

Mr. Barnett studied his little book a few minutes. "Here it is. Last fall two men came. They were Texas Rangers. One said he was thy brother. I told them to come back in the late winter or early spring when Yellow Cloud's band would most likely be here."

Thad kept wondering about Little-bit. "Didn't they say anything about my pony, Little-bit?" he asked.

Mr. Barnett shook his head.

Thad told him how Little-bit had made her way home by herself several times. He added that he wondered why she could not have taken Melissa safely home.

"I don't think it is strange," Mr. Barnett said. "Melissa might have thought thy pony was heading in the wrong direction and reined her in another."

Thad thought that might be the reason. But then, he had told Melissa positively to let Little-bit have her way.

"There are some of our people in War Hawk's village," Thad told him. "There is an old lady, Mis' Sally Buchanan, and her two little grandsons. They are twins. Then there is a little boy Mis' Sally has taken under her wing. She doesn't know his name except he is 'Willy.' Has anyone asked about them?"

"Mrs. Buchanan's son was here last summer," he said. "They believed their mother must be dead, for they had found no trace of her. There is a little boy listed as missing when his family was massacred in San Saba County less than a year ago. I believe there is an older married sister living in San Antonio."

"I know War Hawk," he said. "I'll see what we can do. Then if anyone comes here from your part of the country, they can take these people home, too. But we had better wait a while unless they are being mistreated. Do thee believe they are being treated badly?"

Thad smiled. "I don't think anyone could mistreat those little boys with Mis' Sally around," he replied. "She was captured when she was a little girl and lived with a Comanche band until she was eight years old. She knows their language and she knows how to get along with them."

Mrs. Barnett was a wonderful cook. Thad was not at all sure he was making any headway paying back the $70, because he stuffed himself with her good food three times a day.

"Mr. Barnett," she remarked one morning as she watched him cram food into his lean body, "did thee ever see a boy fill out faster than Thad here?"

His eyes twinkled. "He was so bony when he first came to us

that thee feared his folk would not acknowledge him. Now I suppose they would not know him for his fatness."

A week later an Indian boy who worked at the trading post stuck his head around the corner of the house and called to Thad. "Mr. Barnett says to come. He wants to talk to you."

Thad hurried to the front of the building. Several Indians were lounging on the porch. There were eight or nine horses tied to the hitching post. Looking them over as he had a habit of doing, Thad saw that two of them carried Texas saddles with the Rangers' brand. As he stepped inside, he saw two men talking with Mr. Barnett. Thad's heart turned a somersault; he knew them both.

"Giles!" he yelled, throwing himself at the first one. Giles grabbed him by the shoulders.

Thad turned to the other man. "Howdy, Mr. Johnny!" he greeted.

It was Mr. Johnny Ainsworth. He squinted his one good eye at Thad and said, "Well, young'un, those Comanches haven't been treating you as bad as they did me. You're as fat as a porcupine."

Tears stood in Giles's eyes as he said, "Young'un, you've been long gone from home. Let's get back there, what do you say?"

Both men were bronzed and lean from long riding in the open. Thad could not speak. Giles held him from him a moment, looking him over.

"Law, Thad, you must have grown a foot! You sure enough don't look like those Indians have been mistreating you."

He glanced at Mr. Barnett, who stood smiling. "Mr. Barnett tells me you were right poor and weak when they got hold of you."

Thad nodded. "I had been sick," he said. "The Comanches didn't treat me badly, though. I always did what they told me, like Mr. Johnny said. Why didn't you-all find me before?"

"Pretty hard to find a needle in a haystack, young'un," Giles said. "That's big country out there."

"We had a fight with Yellow Cloud's Indians because we thought you might be among them," Mr. Johnny said. "Why didn't we find you then? We searched the camp."

Thad gasped. "Were you-all there?"

Thad told them what he remembered of the battle and how he had been hidden under a pile of buffalo robes. He mentioned the old woman who sat on top of them to fool the Long Knives.

"Well, I'll be!" Giles exclaimed. "I saw that poor old squaw lying there on a pile of buffalo robes, and almost made her get up. But she seemed so helpless and old that I didn't have the heart to bother her."

Thad told them about Melissa and Little-bit.

"Great day in the morning, young'un! You were over three hundred miles from home! There's no telling what happened to poor little Lissy." He had a worried look.

"Didn't Little-bit ever get home?"

Giles shook his head. "Not yet, she hasn't," he said.

"I heard there's a girl in a Tonkawa camp," Thad said. "Name of the chief is Willowbird. But nobody knows where his camp is."

"Well, that's interesting!" Giles exclaimed. "If the girl is still alive, we'll find her."

"You recollect old Mis' Sally Buchanan who lived up on Windy Creek?" Thad asked.

"Sure, I've known her all my life," Giles said. "She was carried off and killed by Comanches. Her and Buck Buchanan's little twin boys."

"Yes, only they didn't get killed," Thad told him.

"No?" Giles exclaimed. "Everybody in the whole country thought they were carried off and killed. Come to think of it, their bodies never were found."

"I reckon," said Mr. Johnny, "everybody figured Mis' Sally was too old and those little boys too young to live through what those Comanches might do to them."

"I talked to Mis' Sally just before I came here," Thad told them. "She didn't care much about herself, she said. She's getting old and hasn't got her husband anymore, so she doesn't care much if she dies there. That's what she said. But she's terrible worried about those little boys."

"Are they getting bad handling?" Giles asked.

"No, but they're growing up talking Comanche. White Clover, War Hawk's wife, thinks they're her young'uns, just about. She pets them like they were really her own. Mis' Sally doesn't like that at all, and she's anxious for her folks to find them."

"I suppose she would never have lived through it all," Mr. Johnny said, "if she hadn't grown up with them. You get to know how to handle them."

"She's in War Hawk's village," Thad told them. "Mr. Barnett says War Hawk comes in here quite often. Mis' Sally has another little white boy, too. Name's Willy, that's all. Mr. Barnett thinks he comes from San Saba County. His family was massacred."

"War Hawk, huh?" Mr. Johnny said. "I grew up with War Hawk. It was his daddy's outfit that captured me. Name was Walking Bear. I'll have a talk with Mr. War Hawk."

Mr. Barnett warned, "I suppose thee knows thee are only a little more safe with the Indians here in the Territory than in west Texas?"

"I reckon I ought to know those horse thieves pretty well, sir," Mr. Johnny said, pointing to his scarred face and patch-covered eye.

"Are not thee afraid to go among them alone?"

"No, sir, I think I know how to handle them." He glared so fiercely that Thad could hardly believe it was Mr. Johnny.

"I'll tell Mr. War Hawk that Giles and I and our Rangers will hound him till the yellow cows come home. He knows me and he knows the Texas Rangers. He'll turn Mis' Sally and all three of those little boys loose."

Mr. Johnny seemed very sure of himself.

"Well, get on your horse and let's get going," Giles said. "Thad and I are anxious to get back home, aren't we, Thad?"

"I am, for one," Thad said. "But I do want you to get Mis' Sally and those little boys away from the Comanches first."

"We'll do it. You be getting yourself ready to travel."

Then Thad remembered something else. "Oh, I forgot. I owe Mr. Barnett $70."

"Seventy dollars! What is that for?" Giles pretended not to understand. "Is it for board?"

"Oh, no, I've been working for board," Thad explained. "But I belong to Mr. Barnett. He bought me for $70."

"Why, that old skunk!" Giles exclaimed. "Yellow Cloud starved you and beat you and worked you half to death. Then he sold you for cash!" He looked at Thad and grinned.

"Well, I reckon I'm willing to pay $70 to get you home. It will be worth it to see ma's face when you ride in. But you don't look to be worth more than 35 cents on the hoof right now, you young maverick!" He fished the money out of his wallet and handed it to Mr. Barnett.

"There, now," he said to Thad. "You're the Conways' boy again. That suit you?"

Thad's heart was too full for words. Just one thing still worried him now. Would they ever find Melissa and Little-bit?

"I'm to blame if Lissy is dead," he said. "I was the cause of her leaving the Indian camp. She might have lived like I did if she had stayed with them."

"Now, now, son," Mrs. Barnett comforted. "She would probably never have lived through what thee did. Thou art a big, strong boy. Now I think thee will locate her in a village of the Tonkawas."

Mr. Johnny agreed. "There isn't a doubt that she is being taken care of by the Tonkawas. They're friendly to the white folk because we protect them from the Comanches. Now all we've got to do is find the village of old Willowbird."

The men rode off and Mrs. Barnett helped Thad get his belongings ready to start home.

"Six hundred miles is a long way to ride a horse," she said. "I want thee to save one clean outfit to put on before reaching home, so thy mother will not think I have neglected thee."

Giles and Mr. Johnny came back about nine o'clock that night. Mis' Sally and the twins were with them, as was little Willy. They had bought several horses from War Hawk for Thad, Mis' Sally, and the children to ride.

Spotted Boy and the Comanches

Mr. Johnny said, "I think I know the family of this little fellow. They were in a colony of German settlers. Only an older married daughter is still living."

How had they managed to talk White Clover into giving up the twins? Thad wanted to know.

"I don't know much of the Comanche talk," said Giles. "Johnny did the negotiating. He and War Hawk seemed like two old friends getting together."

Mr. Johnny laughed and said, "I knew I could handle War Hawk. He didn't give me any trouble. Cost me $50 for each of them, but I figure I'll get it back. I felt a little sorry for White Clover, though. She was sure attached to those twins, and pretty fond of Willy, too. But she has a young one of her own now, so she'll get over it."

Mis' Sally took a bath the first thing and cleaned up the three little boys. She put on some clothes Mrs. Barnett gave her from the donation barrel.

"Land o' Goshen!" Mis' Sally exclaimed. "I never expected to be going home again. But I did pray the Lord wouldn't leave these little ones to grow up Comanches."

The next morning before the spring sun was up they were packed and ready to start. Some of Mrs. Barnett's good food was in their saddlebags.

"We must have prayer," Mr. Barnett said. It was a comfort to Thad to hear the good man asking God to go with them on their journey and to see them safely home. Then he prayed that Melissa might be found.

Mrs. Barnett kissed Thad and Mis' Sally and the little boys goodbye. Mr. Barnett patted Thad on the back. "He is a good boy," he said to Giles, "and I'm sure that only his trust in God brought him through."

Afterward Thad was never quite sure whether he remembered to thank God for taking care of him. Sometimes a boy is good at asking, but not so good at saying "Thank you."

Home at Last

15

THOUGH it was springtime, the journey home was a cold and hungry one. For two weeks the little party traveled, much of the time in the rain. They stopped at the Buchanan ranch one rainy night. Mis' Sally got stiffly down from her horse, and her daughter-in-law, Mis' Laurie, came on the run. At first she did not recognize the two robe-wrapped bundles, one on Mis' Sally's saddle, the other on Giles's. The little fellows were sound asleep. Willy was asleep in Mr. Johnny's arms. Mr. Johnny had petted and coddled him the whole trip.

"I kind of feel a kinship to the little feller," he said. "He's a poor little orphan like I was."

When Mis' Laurie discovered the contents of the bundles and the little boys came pushing out of the robes, she snatched one of them while her husband, Buck, took the other. Thad's eyes filled with tears at the joyful reunion. For all the Buchanans knew, the three of them had been dead for almost two years.

Mis' Laurie was hysterical. "Oh, ma, ma!" she cried, throwing her arms about her mother-in-law. "You saved them! You saved our babies!"

Mr. Buck chuckled dryly. "Might have known it would take more than a passel of wild Comanches to get the best of our ma," he said.

Mis' Sally grinned impishly. "I didn't reckon you put that much faith in your ma, son."

As they rode in to the home place the next evening, the house and barns, huddled in the cold rain, had never looked so good to Thad. The riders struck spurs to their tired horses as they rode down the lane.

The horses were glad to be at home, too, and needed no urging. They splashed through the mud, the men waving their hats and giving forth with Comanche yells. They were sure that

Mis' Laurie came running out to meet them. At first she did
not recognize the robe-wrapped bundles. Then she snatched
up one of the little boys. It was a joyful reunion for all!

would bring the family running, and it did. Pa, ma, Travis, Dulcie, and little Stevie came hurrying from the house as the travelers rode up to the kitchen door.

Thad was afraid his mother would faint when she first saw him. No one had told her that Giles and Mr. Johnny had gone to the Territory to look for him.

"Why didn't you-all tell me where you were going?" she demanded of Giles after she had come close to cracking Thad's ribs with her hugging.

"We figured that you and pa have had enough disappointments already, and we didn't know for sure we'd find him," Giles explained.

They told the family all they knew of Mis' Sally, the twins, and the rumors of a white girl in Willowbird's Tonkawa village. They also presented the little blond boy, Willy.

Pa said, "Well, now at last we've heard something more promising than anything before."

Ma said, "Dulcie and I will take care of Willy until we can find his sister."

"This young one is my own personal affair," Mr. Johnny said. "If you'll take him over till I can locate his sister, I'll see that he gets home to her."

"When are we going to try to find Willowbird's village?" Thad asked impatiently. He knew the Tonkawas were enemies of the Comanches, and usually friendly to the white people.

"Maybe it was some other white girl the Tonkawas found," Thad suggested. He could hardly let himself hope that they had found a trace of Melissa.

"Not much chance that there was any other white girl riding alone across west Texas on a black pony," Giles responded. "I have a feeling we're getting a lead on Melissa's whereabouts."

"Why doesn't somebody do something about it, then?" Thad demanded. He was of a mind to get on a horse and start out in the rain.

"Don't worry, son. We sent word to Wiley Branson as soon as

you told us about those Tonkawa scouts. He'll be here and Beau with him as soon as they can make it."

Thad had to be satisfied with that.

Wiley Branson had built a small cabin alongside the Conways' house, where Aunt Dulcie and little Steve could stay until he could get his family together again. He and Beau stayed there, too, when they were not out searching for Melissa. At that time they were away looking for her, following up a rumor.

Stevie was fat and healthy and as happy as a little boy could be. Aunt Dulcie had to hear all about Melissa. She wanted to know how the Comanches dressed her, how they treated her, and most of all, how she got away from them. Tears ran down her cheeks as Thad talked.

"Oh, my baby!" she wailed. "When they goin' to find my Lissy? We done los' Mis' Marcella and little Celie. When they goin' to bring back my Lissy?"

Wiley Branson and Beau arrived a day or so later and were quite excited to hear the Tonkawa story. They set out the next day, hoping to find the Tonkawa camp.

From the first Thad missed the affectionate nicker of Little-bit. Never since he had first got her had she failed to welcome him except when she had been away with the Comanches.

Aside from that, Thad's first morning at home seemed as near heaven as he ever hoped to have on this earth. He had slept all night in his own warm feather bed. He had awakened to the smell of breakfast cooking: eggs frying and ma's feather-light biscuits browning in the oven. He put on the clean clothes ma had laid out for him to wear, some of Travis's old ones. His own clothes would be far too small. He hurried to the kitchen, where ma had the breakfast almost ready.

Ma sent him to the well to bring in the cold milk as she always had. It was a delight for him to watch his mother that morning, and to sniff the odors of home. It was pure joy to eat the good victuals she cooked, after pa and Travis had brought in foaming buckets of milk and ma had strained it.

For days Thad took pleasure in the life at home. Like any boy, he had not appreciated it so much before. If his long months with the Comanches had accomplished nothing else, they had helped him love his home more.

One morning after breakfast ma looked lovingly at Thad for a while. Then she said, "It was worth it, honey. I'm glad we made you do it."

"What was worth it, ma? What did you make me do?"

"Honey, you used to buck like a bay steer at having to learn all those Scripture texts. You know you did. But you'll have to admit that they brought you home to us."

Thad knew what she meant, and he felt the same way about it. Besides, the Bible texts had helped him obey patiently instead of fighting against the Indians. If he had resisted them, things might have turned out far different. They had helped him in another way, too. Never again would he feel hatred for another person. Now he hated only the Indians' evil actions, and he regarded those actions as the result of wrong thinking. He had learned to love some individuals among them, for the same reasons that he loved certain white folk. He wished only good for all of them.

Then he thought of Melissa. "We'll find Melissa, too," he said.

"I've been sure of that ever since our prayers have been answered by your homecoming," ma agreed.

Thad sat thinking for some time. "I got to where I sort of loved Little Rabbit like I love you," he said. "I remembered listening to Mr. Lafe Allen arguing with Preacher Heston. He claimed he could never love a Comanche, and I felt the same way. Of course, even though I loved Little Rabbit sort of in the same way I love you, especially after I was sick and she took such good care of me, I never loved her so much. And I loved Scar Pony sort of like I love Travis."

"In her own way Little Rabbit is a good woman, no doubt," ma said. "I'd like to get to know her."

"I had just about come to the place where I could love Yellow Cloud, too. Then I saw the cameo."

"Cameo?" ma asked. "He had a cameo?"

Thad nodded. "It was a broochpin. It had a letter 'M' worked into the rim in the gold part. He wore it around his neck when he put on his war clothes along with a lot of other stuff—beads, bear claws, a gold watch, and such things. I got a good look at it when he was putting them on. He hung the pin on a rawhide thong. It was Mis' Marcella Branson's pin."

Ma caught a quick breath.

"Oh, son!" was all she said.

*   *   *

Wiley and Beau Branson rode in after a week or so. Thad knew as soon as he saw them getting off their horses at the lot that they had not found Melissa. They had simply not been able to locate Willowbird's village. The Tonkawas had apparently been on the move for the past few months, and no one knew where to look for them.

They planned to start again in a few days when early one morning two riders came to the Conway ranch. Thad was out at the lot stacking hay when they rode in. He recognized one of them as Mis' Sally's son Buck, the father of the twins. He was anxious to know why they had come.

"Your pa around?" Buck asked. Mr. Conway came from the barn just then.

"Here I am," he said.

"We're really looking for Wiley Branson," Buck said.

"He's in our house right now," Mr. Conway told him. "Have you got good news for him?"

"We think so," Buck replied.

They hurried to the house, Thad following them. He was all atremble to hear what the men had to say. Somehow he felt as though the news would be good this time. Wiley Branson must have felt the same way. He was more excited than anyone had seen him before.

"Don't send me on any more wild-goose chases," he begged them. "What's your news?"

"I don't believe this is a wild-goose chase, Mr. Branson," Buck said. "We went to Fort Concho day before yesterday. They told us that a couple of Tonkawas from Willowbird's village had visited the fort. The Indians said their chief had heard that the Long Knives were searching for a white girl. They had come to lead the Rangers to Willowbird's village. Captain Howard had sent two of his men with the Tonkawas to bring the girl to the fort. If they succeeded, all you need to do is go to Fort Concho."

"I'll be ready to ride in twenty minues," Wiley Branson said. "Come on, Beau, get your things together."

"I'm going, too." Thad could scarcely recognize his own voice. He ran to saddle up Git-along, a buckskin he had been riding in place of Little-bit. Mother Conway went to the kitchen to get some rations for the journey.

Father Conway's voice was quieter and steadier than Thad's. "I'll go with you, too, Wiley," he said.

Melissa Returns

16

A S THEY traveled all that day, Thad was keyed up with excitement. His brothers and Wiley Branson had investigated dozens of leads like this, and none of them had led to rescue. But they felt that this one could be different. This time Thad, at least, was certain they would find Melissa.

They reached Fort Concho the following afternoon and rode into the stockade. The soldiers were gone now, but the fort was held by a company of Texas Rangers. A sentry asked their business.

"Tell your commanding officer we heard he has located a white girl in Willowbird's village," Wiley Branson replied.

In a minute or so a Ranger captain invited them in. Wiley Branson, Beau, Thad, and Thad's father followed them into his office.

"I'm right sorry to tell you, Mr. Branson, that we did not find your girl," the man said.

"Have you been to Willowbird's camp?" Wiley asked.

"Day before yesterday. I sent two of our men to talk to Willowbird and bring the girl here. Willowbird swore up and down that she wasn't there. He said they had traded her to some Comanches for two ponies a while back."

"Do you believe that?" Wiley asked him.

"No, sir, I don't," Captain Howard answered. "I'm as sure as I am standing here that your little girl is still with Willowbird's people. He's probably decided he wants to keep her for some reason and is stalling us."

"Tell me how I can get to his camp and I'll fetch her if I have to whip Willowbird's whole village singlehanded." Wiley's voice was bitter. "I'm tired of this rousting around all over west Texas hunting for my girl and those Indians laughing in my face."

"We'll go with you, Wiley," father Conway said.

144

"I'll go, too. I can spare about fifteen men to go along," Captain Howard promised.

"How far away is the village?" pa asked.

"We can leave after dinner and make it before sundown," Captain Howard said. "I don't expect them to put up a fight when they see we mean business. But you never can tell about an Indian. The Tonkawas help us Rangers a lot. That's because they hate the Comanches, not because they think much of us. Willowbird has had several run-ins with white men, mostly over stealing horses."

Git-along, the tough, wiry buckskin pony Thad was riding, was faster than most of the Conway riding stock. He was one of the best cow ponies they had. Thad hoped to find Little-bit if she could be found, and he wanted a fast horse to outrun the others if he should need to race the Indians for her. Captain Howard had said nothing about trying to recover a certain little black pony with a scissors-shaped scar on her hip, but Thad was determined to bring her home if she was in the camp of the Tonkawas.

They rode all afternoon in a northwesterly direction. Finally, when the rays of the sun were slanting long across the prairie toward them, they sighted dust.

Topping a rise, they saw the Tonkawas coming on the next ridge. They were strung out without order or anything like a fighting line. It was every man for himself. The Tonkawas were riding like Jehu and yelling like a pack of hounds hot on the trail of a fox. Beyond them could be seen the smoke of village fires.

The Indians kept coming toward the white men and the white men headed straight for them. There were about twice as many Tonkawas as rangers, Thad estimated.

The rangers split into parties of two or three to meet the scattered Tonkawas and keep from being surrounded. It looked as though they had an unexpected battle on their hands. But for some reason the Indians had not shot an arrow. They were painted for battle and carried their bows with arrows nocked. But not a warrior raised his bow.

Then a chief, the breeze fingering the eagle feathers in his elegant war bonnet, rode from the group. He held up his hand in the sign for parley. The chief was Willowbird.

Captain Howard signaled his men to hold their fire while he rode ahead to meet the old chief. Thad was fidgety. He knew how long and ceremonious such a council among Indians could be. He was anxious to get the whole thing settled, and to see Melissa and take her home.

Captain Howard and Willowbird talked and talked as Thad knew they would. After what seemed a very long time, he became so restless that he felt he could not take any more waiting. He scanned the area about the camp and along the creek where the village was located, hoping to find the horse herd. Finally he saw it beyond the creek.

Slipping away through the thick growth of timber, while all eyes were focused on the palaver between the Ranger and Chief Willowbird, he rode between the high banks of the creek. There he tethered Git-along.

Creeping up the opposite bank, he watched the horses for a while, trying to locate Little-bit. For minutes that seemed like an hour, he watched them grazing, but could not locate his pony.

A shrill whinny cut the air and drew his eyes to a commotion on the far edge of the grazing herd. It was Little-bit! She had recognized him; how, he would never know. She came hobbling toward him. He ran as fast as he could toward her, scattering the surprised horses. She nickered eagerly, thrusting her muzzle into his hand. He hugged her neck and then cut her hobbles.

He leaped to his pony's back and rode her to the creek. There he put his lasso rope around her neck. If there were any horse guards with the herd, he had not seen them, nor had they discovered him. Perhaps they, too, were curiously watching the palaver going on outside the village.

Leading Little-bit, he rode to the outskirts of the bargaining party and watched proceedings from the shelter of the timber.

He watched until he saw Willowbird send a messenger into

the village. In a few moments he saw the brave return with a middle-aged woman and a girl. His heart was pounding with anticipation. This girl must be Melissa. He was sure she was when he saw her passed to Willowbird, who led her to Captain Howard. Thad began edging toward the captain now, leading his pony.

Melissa was taller and thinner than when he had last seen her. She seemed dazed. Even when she recognized her father and Beau, she stood looking at them with an air of embarrassment.

Her father took her in his arms and kissed her. "Lissy, Lissy, my baby!" he murmured over and over while Beau patted her awkwardly on the shoulder.

Captain Howard handed money to Chief Willowbird. Evidently it was the price agreed upon for Melissa's ransom. Mr. Branson had given it to the captain for that purpose.

Thad decided this was the time to press his own claim, so he rode up to the group leading Little-bit.

"I have brought the girl's pony," he said to Captain Howard. "Will you ransom her, too?"

Captain Howard looked from Thad to his father and then to Wiley Branson. Thad's father took in the situation and stepped forward. "I'll ransom the pony," he said. "How much?"

The chief held up the fingers of both hands and seemed disappointed when his father paid the ten dollars without bargaining. He had missed half the fun of the deal.

"It was worth $10 to end that everlasting dickering," father Conway said. He rode beside Thad as they started back toward the fort.

Wiley Branson and Beau, with Melissa riding between them, caught up with Thad and his father in a few moments.

"Howdy, Lissy," Thad greeted her, grinning.

She looked him over as though she didn't recognize him. Then she replied, "Oh Thad, I didn't think I'd ever see you again!"

Thad's eyes were shining as he reined his horse alongside hers.

"We've got a lot to talk about, Lissy, when we get to the fort. I've a thousand questions to ask you."

148

"I want to ask you some, too," she said. Then the whole party fell into a steady, mile-eating pace. But Thad, riding behind the Bransons, kept Melissa constantly in view. He felt that he must never let her out of his sight again.

"Those Tonkawas didn't want a battle any more than we did," Captain Howard said, laughing as he dismounted at the fort. "One of their braves had taken a shine to Melissa and wanted her for his squaw. Old Willowbird thought he could bluff us into believing he had traded her. He'd have been talking yet if I hadn't threatened to destroy his village."

*   *   *

Mrs. Howard had taken Melissa over as soon as she got to the fort. When Thad and his father entered, they were told to wait for her. Wiley and Beau were waiting, too. Soon Melissa came into the room accompanied by Mrs. Howard. She was dressed in a pink calico instead of the ragged doeskin squaw dress she had been wearing before.

Whenever Thad was outdoors, Little-bit kept as close to him as she could get. She would lay her head on his shoulder and nicker softly.

The following day the Bransons and the Conways started home. At first Thad left Melissa with her father and brother. Wiley wore a happy grin most of the day. Every little while he would say, "Lissy, my little girl, my baby! You finally came back."

The second day of their homeward travel Thad rode beside Melissa some of the time. They laughed over the things that had happened to them in Yellow Cloud's camp. Thad had to tell her why he was never able to catch up with her after they heard the Indians chasing them. He explained how he had turned so that they would follow him instead of Melissa. But she had guessed all that.

Melissa found it difficult to express her thoughts in English at first, so long had she spoken in the tongues of the Comanches and the Tonkawas. But Thad got her to tell the story of what had happened after she had left him that morning. He was anxious to learn why Little-bit had not managed to bring her directly home.

"Oh, that was my fault," Melissa said. "You told me to let her have her head. But one day I thought we were lost. I reckon I wasn't just right in my own head by then. I kept pulling her to the left when she wanted to go to the right. That's when we really got lost, I guess."

"Was it then that the Tonkawas found you?"

"I don't remember seeing them," she said. "By that time I was so sick that the first thing I remember was when I came to my senses in their village. I was in one of their little brush wickiups. But I thought it was a tepee. That made me think I was in Yellow Cloud's camp again. There was only one person in the village who could speak a little English, but some of them could speak Comanche. So I found out where I was."

Mrs. Conway and Dulcie did everything love could do to help Melissa forget the hardships she had been through. It seemed for the first few weeks that she took greater comfort in being with Stevie than with any of the others. He was a bright, good-humored little fellow, and he had been his sister's special pet since the day he was born.

There was something Thad was anxious to find out about: "How come Little-bit stayed with Willowbird's horse herd instead of heading home when she got a chance?"

"They staked her out every night," Melissa told him, "and they hobbled her every day. They thought she was my pony, so they were keeping her for me."

"Would you like her?" Thad asked.

"Would I like what?" Melissa did not understand what he was leading up to.

"Would you like Little-bit to be your pony?" Thad said.

A smile lighted her face. "Oh, I'd love to have her for my own," she said. "I love that pony! If it hadn't been for her, I might still be with the Comanches or dead somewhere on the prairie."

"You can have her," Thad said. "From now on she's your pony."

Never before had Thad felt so much pleasure in giving away a cherished possession. He loved both the girl and the pony with all his heart.

"But you love Little-bit as much as I do," Melissa protested. "I really should not take her."

"Oh, I'm getting too long-legged for a little pony like her," Thad explained, as though that were the real reason.

When Thad was twenty years old, Little-bit was once again
in his possession. After Thad and Melissa married and had
a family, the horse was also loved by the Conway children.

Back Along the Trail   17

RAIDS by the Comanches continued along the Texas
frontier for another fifteen years, but they lessened
in frequency and violence. While serving with the Texas Rangers
for several years, Thad Conway did his part in ending the Indian
raids.

If any braves of Yellow Cloud's band were among those who
attacked the Conway's Double Bar O Ranch on several occasions,
Thad never knew of it. Scar Pony kept the promise he had made
that Little-bit would not be stolen again.

When Thad was twenty years old, Little-bit came once again into
his possession. It was then that he and Melissa were married. The
rest of their lives Melissa jokingly insisted that the only reason
Thad married her was to get back his pony.

When Thad had built up a herd of his own, he chose an open
pair of scissors like the scar on Little-bit as his brand. Cattlemen
far and near came to know the Scissors Ranch and to respect the
quality of the cattle that bore Thad's brand. But few ever knew
the origin of the mark.

*   *   *

Finally the day came when Thad retired from ranching and
gave his herds and lands to his eldest son, young Giles. One day
when Giles was opening his mail, he exclaimed, "Dad, did you
know a Comanche boy named Scar Pony?"

"Yes, son, I did," Thad answered. "He was my best friend among
the Comanches."

"Here's a letter from Oklahoma," Giles told him, "asking for
some of our best breeding stock. It is signed, 'Leonard Scar-Pony.'
Might be kin to your old pal."

"Why, of course, son, it has to be. No doubt it is Scar Pony's
son. I'd love to see old Scar Pony. I heard that he took over as
chief of the band after Yellow Cloud died. Could have had that

153

Spotted Boy and the Comanches

job myself, I reckon, if I'd stayed with them." He chuckled with amusement at the thought.

"Well, dad, I'll be taking a shipment of cows to this Leonard Scar-Pony in a couple of weeks. How about coming along?"

So it came about that Thad Conway and Scar Pony met once more. They no longer considered themselves enemies, and Thad was amazed at the changes in the Comanche manner of life. No longer raiders and killers, they were living peacefully on farms and ranches, sending sons and daughters to school and building houses.

Leonard Scar-Pony, he was told, was a leader in his tribe and was helping build up the quality of the Indians' cattle. He was a graduate of an agricultural college, and had heard of the cattle with the famous Scissors brand.

Scar Pony had accepted the white man's style of dress in only a few particulars. He wore a hat with the crown high and uncrushed, with a feather in the band. His hair was cut short like the white man's. Indian buckskin shirt, above white man's trousers plus beaded moccasins, completed his dress. He still preferred to live in the portable buffalo-hide lodge of his ancestors beside a creek, though his children had built houses for their families.

"I am deacon in the church," Scar Pony told him. "We no longer fear the spirits. Many of us worship as you do. We honor the Father-God and His Son, who loves both Indians and white men. Now we teach the young of our tribe to love, not to hate."

"I'm glad to hear that," Thad told him. "How did it come about?"

"Missionaries from many churches come and teach Comanches about this God and this Book. Then I remember what you tell me many years ago. You tell us to love our enemies, not hate them. These things I believe. It is good truth. Has made my family very happy."

And so the old times were recalled and events of those long-ago days lived over in the memories of two old men, one dark, one fair.

* * *

As Thad Conway sat on his front porch, he began to reminisce as Melissa came out to sit beside him.

"Just think of it now," he said. "Scar Pony thinks I taught him to love his enemies, and all the time I was trying my best to hate the Comanches. Guess I didn't do such a good job of hating after all."

"Well, dear," Melissa answered, "hatred does more harm to the vessel that holds it than it does to the one it is poured out upon."

Thad spoke again. "Scar Pony, my enemy, became the best friend of my boyhood—mostly because of Little-bit. Only he called her Blackbird. Both of us loved her."

"All of us loved Little-bit," Melissa said.

They sat for a long time in silence as the shadow of a little black Spanish mare, now long gone, seemed to rise before their eyes.